A Surprise Visitor

Eve dropped me off in front of Paradise Gardens, and I walked through the courtyard toward my building. The light near my stairway had been out for about a week, so it was always a little creepy at night. I usually just started running while I was still near the streetlight and raced through the darkest part until I was at my door.

I was preparing to run, when I heard a noise by the stairs. I looked hard into the darkness and saw the dim outline of a person.

Then the man stepped out of the shadows and I saw h
he w

"

Cover
Kids

Tracey's Tough Choice

Suzanne Weyn

Troll Associates

Tracey's Tough Choice

Chapter One

————◆————

Mom, chill out, would you?"
I cried, shaking my head. My mother stood in front of the
bathroom mirror, running her hands frantically through
her dark blond hair.

"Why didn't you tell me my hair looked this bad,
Tracey?" she asked. "It's like a frizz mop!"

"It doesn't look bad to me," I said as I leaned against
the bathroom doorway and unwrapped a piece of bubble
gum.

My mother began rummaging around in the narrow
bathroom closet. "I know I have some mousse here. That
might tame it," she muttered, tossing things she didn't
want onto the sink.

My mother is big on throwing stuff out of the way and
then forgetting about it. That's probably why our
apartment is always such a wreck—except for my room.

That I keep neat. Not that I'm a neat freak or anything, I just like a little order.

"Here it is!" my mother said, pulling a spray can of mousse from the closet. "I have just enough time to work on it before Mel comes. Now, let me see. What am I supposed to do? Mousse and scrunch, or scrunch and mousse? Is there any difference? I'm no good at this."

"I'll do it," I said, taking the can from her. I pressed the nozzle and white foam came out. Putting some on Mom's head, I scrunched and held her hair a moment, the way I'd seen the hairdresser at the Calico agency do it.

Two months ago, I wouldn't have known a can of hair mousse from Bullwinkle the Moose. But since then, I'd learned a lot. That's because I won a modeling contract with the agency.

Winning it was a super surprise. My cousin Doris was the one who wanted to enter the Calico agency's Model Search Contest at the Appleton Mall. I was just there to keep her company. But the weirdest thing happened. I was the one chosen to be a model!

Life hasn't been the same since.

"We're getting there, Mom," I said as I let go of a handful of bouncy, crinkly curls. "That looks good."

"Thanks, Tracey," Mom said, still fidgeting nervously. "I hope he's not early. No . . . I've never known Mel to be early. He is definitely not the early type."

This was my mother's first date in ages. She and my father were divorced a long, long time ago. Now she was dating Mel, this guy she works with down at the Department of Social Services. He's some kind of counselor. I'd never met him, but she was very excited. "If Mel comes before I'm ready, you be nice to him, okay?" she said. "Offer him some iced tea or something."

"Sure," I answered. "I'll serve him the finest powdered instant in our best jelly-jar glasses."

"Don't be a brat," she said as I scrunched another bunch of hair.

"I'm not being a brat," I defended myself. "I'm just being my naturally witty self."

Mom sighed. "Very funny, wise guy. Take a good glass from the cabinet above the refrigerator." She turned and took the mousse from me. "I think I have the hang of this now. I can finish up. You go out to the living room and listen for the bell."

"You'll look great," I said, patting her shoulder. I left the bathroom and sauntered down the hall. When I reached the living room, I stopped and looked the place over. My mother had cleaned it up, which made it look totally strange. I wasn't used to seeing it in this orderly condition.

One of the reasons our apartment is always such a mess is that my mother works a lot. She doesn't have time to worry about cleaning, and, the truth is, I'm not much help.

My mother is head of foster care for the county. It's a pretty good job, but she works a lot of hours and even weekends sometimes. It's hard to understand why we're always broke, considering how hard she works. I guess that's how it is for a single woman with an almost thirteen-year-old kid.

I plopped into a big chair and ran my hands along the smooth, worn spots on the arms. Just then, the phone on the table beside me rang. "Clancy's Funeral Home," I answered, just for a goof.

"Ha! I know that's you, Tracey."

"Well, I know your voice, too, Nikki," I replied. "So there."

"Do you need a lift in to the agency tomorrow?" asked my friend Nikki Wilton, who is also a model. "Eve is taking me."

"Great," I said. "I got a call this afternoon to interview for some cupcake shoot. The girl they originally wanted got sick or something."

"Cool! This will be your first solo assignment. Are you nervous?" she asked.

"No," I told her. "What are you going in for?"

"Cotton Kids—their spring line. They want some shots at the zoo."

"Sounds like fun," I said.

"Yeah, it should be. See you tomorrow. Come over by eleven, okay?"

"That's perfect," I told her. "Bye."

Nikki and I have gotten to be pretty good friends since we started modeling together. I'm not surprised that we've grown tight. I liked her as soon as I met her when we were in line at the mall for the contest.

I'm glad I'm friends with Nikki, as well as with two other girls, Chloe and Ashley, at the agency. If it wasn't for them, I might not have any friends at all. That's because since I became a model, I have less and less time for my friends at school. Some of the girls I used to hang around with have gotten really annoyed with me. They've stopped coming to my locker in the morning, and they act like I've deserted them. That's not true. It's just that my life has suddenly gotten onto the zoom track.

It's still weird to me that I was one of the winners of the modeling contest. I mean, I understand why Nikki won. She's tall and has long red hair and great big blue eyes. She really looks like a model. But I've never thought of myself as the modeling type.

I think it was my eyes that won it for me. They're a light aqua blue, and they *are* sort of startling. Other than that, I have dark brown hair and I'm five feet, eight inches tall, which I suppose is a model-like quality. Mostly, though, I never thought about my looks too much.

Modeling isn't the kind of thing that would normally appeal to me. Standing around wearing designer clothes makes me feel dumb. I might have blown the whole thing off, except that when I took a look at my prize package, I nearly fainted.

Among a lot of other prizes was a one-year modeling contract. Part of that contract was the promise of a thousand dollars. The agency gave it to new models right up front, before they even went on a job. And after they earned out the thousand, they got to keep the rest of the money they made (minus the agency's share, of course).

I couldn't turn it down. We could sure use the money.

The phone rang again. I figured it was Nikki calling back about something. "Yo, speaking," I answered as I picked up the phone.

The line crackled, but no one spoke. I hate it when stuff like that happens. "If you're some weirdo, you'd better hang up because I have special security caller I.D.," I growled. This was a lie, but whoever was on the phone didn't know that. "Your phone number is blinking on my telephone right now, and it's being electronically transmitted to the cops. Any minute now, they'll be breaking down your door and you'll be in big—"

"Sorry, sorry," said a man's nervous voice. "Is this the Morris household?"

"What's it to you?" I asked. "Who are you? Didn't your mother ever teach you to identify yourself on the phone?"

Since I didn't recognize the voice, I figured it was Mel. It annoyed me that my mother was going out with a guy who lacked basic phone manners.

The man laughed nervously. "Sorry. Is this Tracey?"

"If you don't tell me who you are, I'm hanging up."

"Don't hang up," he said quickly. "This is Dan Morris."

I sucked in my breath sharply. I wasn't expecting that!

Dan Morris is my father's name. The father I've never met because he left my mother while she was still pregnant. My mother says he was a drunken idiot.

"Hello? Hello?" Dan Morris spoke over the line. "Are you still there?"

"Yeah," I said. "How did you get this number?"

"From the phone book."

"Oh, yeah, sure, of course," I said, sounding like a dope.

I can't describe how it felt to be talking to him. In my mind, I didn't have a father. It was as if my mother just had me on her own. At least, that's how I had always thought of it. I'd never wasted any time making up a fantasy father or wishing he'd come around or any useless stuff like that. I simply didn't have a father, and that was that.

Only now I did. And he had a voice.

"This is Tracey, isn't it?" he asked.

"Yeah," I said cautiously.

"I'm sure you must be surprised to hear from me," he went on.

Normally I would have said something like, "No kidding, Einstein." But right now I was too stunned to be witty.

"I'm in town and I'd like to come over and see you," he said. "I think we can really have a chance to get to know each other. Is your mother there? I'd like to speak—"

That was all I heard because I gently hung up the

phone. Almost instantly it began to ring again, but I picked it up and plunked it back down.

My mother came tearing out of the bathroom with half a head of scrunched hair. "I heard the phone. Was that Mel?"

"No, it was Dan Morris," I told her.

"What?" she cried.

"Yep, big Dan the man himself," I replied, regaining some of my cool.

"What did he want?"

"To see me."

"What did you say?" she asked.

"I hung up on him. He was about to ask to talk to you. Do you want to talk to him?"

She sat on the arm of the couch as if someone had just knocked the air out of her. "No...I don't know. Maybe...I can't believe he's calling after all these years! How did he sound?"

"I don't know," I replied. "Normal and all."

"He wasn't, uh . . . ?"

"He didn't sound drunk, if that's what you mean," I said. "Don't worry, Mom. I'm not going to see him."

"Are you sure that's what you want? Not to see him?" she asked. "He wasn't a bad guy when he was sober. You might want to get to know him."

I sensed that my mother was just trying to be fair. I don't think she really adored the idea of Dan Morris coming back into our lives.

"I haven't needed him for almost thirteen years," I told her. "Now I'm almost grown and all the work is done."

"You're not almost grown," she said.

"Am so," I shot back.

At that moment, the doorbell rang. From the way my mother jumped, you'd have thought a firecracker had gone off under her robe. "It's him! It's him!" she said in a panicky whisper. "Tell him I'll be right out."

"Will do," I said. I waited until my mother was safely in the bathroom before I headed to the door. But first I took my sunglasses off the table and put them on. I have this thing about sunglasses. I like to wear them whenever I'm not entirely comfortable with a situation.

I opened the door and saw a guy in his forties. He was tall, with a neatly trimmed beard, and wore a blue down jacket. "Hi, I'm Mel Nowinski," he said.

"Hi," I said, stepping aside so he could come in. "Mom will be out in a minute."

He stood, clapping his gloved hands together and looking around the place, probably admiring the tidiness. Boy, was he in for a rude awakening if he got to know the *real* Mom! He shot me an odd glance. It was probably the sunglasses.

"My mother's still getting ready. Want some iced tea?" I asked.

"I wouldn't mind some hot tea," he replied. "It's cold out there."

I didn't feel like bothering, but, contrary to what my

mother said, I'm not a brat. I dug through the kitchen pantry until I found a tea bag. Then I stuck it in a cup with water and put it in the microwave for two minutes.

I glanced at Mel waiting in the living room. He didn't seem particularly handsome. What was Mom all flipped out about? If this was her idea of good-looking, I couldn't imagine what my father looked like. I'd never seen a picture of him. Mom said they couldn't even afford a camera back then.

"You could take off your jacket if you want, Mr. Nowinski," I offered.

"Sure, thanks. Call me Mel."

From the bathroom, I heard the sound of the blow-dryer just as the microwave beeped. I guess Mom had decided she couldn't scrunch fast enough to do the rest of her hair, so she was blowing out her half-scrunched side. "Here's your tea," I said, bringing it to Mel.

He took the tea and sat in a living room chair. "I hear you're a model. How do you like it?"

"I'm not sure yet," I answered honestly. "There's a lot about it that's dopey, but I've met some cool girls, and you wouldn't believe how much you get paid."

"That sounds good," he said, dunking his tea bag up and down in the cup.

"The money part is good," I agreed. "It takes up a lot of time, though, and there are other things I might like to do."

"So I hear. Your mother says you're a fine student."

"I guess you could say that," I admitted.

"So, do you enjoy being gifted?" Mel asked.

What kind of question was that? "I suppose," I said.

"That's good, because some young people feel uncomfortable about their intelligence."

"Uh-huh," I said, trying to stifle a yawn. This guy was really boring!

Just then my mother appeared, trailing a cloud of sweet perfume. She was wearing a flowing, embroidered black top over her good jeans. She'd tied her hair back in a braid. I thought she looked really pretty in a hippie sort of way.

Mel stood. "Hi, Caroline. You look lovely."

Finally she and Mel left on their date. The apartment was full of Mom's perfume. I didn't particularly love the smell, so I went outside to get some air.

Mom and I live in the Paradise Gardens Apartments. Each building has a porch that runs in front of all the apartments on the second floor. That's where I like to sit and think.

I was just standing there when I heard this weird whimpering sound. I walked to the end of our porch and took off my sunglasses. Down at the bottom of the outside stairs was this little gray dog. "What's the matter, you little mop?" I said as I went down toward him.

The dog acted like he knew me, even though he didn't. He started jumping around happily. There was no collar on his neck, and he was really dirty and skinny. I got the feeling he didn't belong to anybody.

I scooped him up and brought him into the apartment. "You'd better be quiet," I warned him. "We're not allowed to have pets here." I put him down and he danced around on the carpet. There were two hard-boiled eggs in the refrigerator, so I peeled them and he gobbled them up, his tail wagging.

It sure is simple to make dogs happy. They don't have moms and dads who complicate their lives.

Chapter Two

———◆———

The next day, Nikki and I were barely two steps into the hallway of the Calico agency when our friend Ashley Taylor came steaming out of Kate Calico's office like an express train. Her brows were knitted, and her long blond wavy hair bounced behind her as she came toward us.

"What's the matter?" Nikki asked.

"Kate is the matter!" she said, referring to Kate Calico, the head of the agency. "She told me I'm not old enough to be the California Essence perfume girl."

"So, what's the big deal?" I asked, taking off my sunglasses. Ashley is one of the most successful junior models at the agency. For the most part, she gets whatever job she wants.

"The big deal is—" Ashley cut herself short as a tall black girl of about sixteen came out of Ms. Calico's office.

19

It was Brittany Wells, the agency's top model.

Ashley shot Brittany a cold look, but Brittany just smiled serenely. That's the only expression I've ever seen on her face.

"Come on," Ashley said to us as Brittany glided down the hall. "Let's talk where no one can hear us."

Nikki and I both knew where she was headed: to the Red Room. It's a photographer's dark room at the end of a quiet hallway. The room has red light because it was used only by Kate Calico's photographer/filmmaker husband. He told Ms. Calico he was most creative in red light. But Mr. Calico never uses the room anymore, and everyone's kind of forgotten it. Ashley discovered it one day. Now she, Nikki, Chloe Chang, and I use the room as our secret place when we need a break, want to study, or have something important to discuss.

When we were inside, Ashley flicked on the light. In the red glow, her brown eyes looked almost black. "The big deal is that I need this job so I can go to California and spend some time with my dad."

"But what about the movie deal?" Nikki asked. "I thought that was going forward."

Ashley's mother is the television talk-show host Taylor Andrews. Her half brother, John Renee, is on the series "One Ashford Avenue" with other teen heartthrobs. Her parents are divorced and her father is a director out in Hollywood.

"The movie is off," Ashley said angrily. "John's agent,

who was supposed to be working everything out for me, said they decided to cut the role I was up for."

"Bummer," I said. I knew how much Ashley had hoped to get that part. Even though she was really successful as a model, she'd never acted.

"Super bummer," Ashley agreed. "Mom is going to be in Brazil for most of December filming some documentary on the rain forest. That means I'll be all alone for the holidays."

"Wouldn't your father invite you to visit him?" Nikki asked.

"Yeah, but then I'd have to leave again. If I had a job out there, I'd have a reason to stay with him for a while," Ashley said. "I'd like to do that. I miss him."

"Do you need a reason just to stay with your father?" Nikki asked delicately. "I mean, he is your father, after all."

Ashley frowned and slid down the wall onto the tile floor. "It's a touchy subject with my mom," Ashley said. "Even though she's never home, she still has custody of me. If I just went out to see Dad for no reason, she'd think I was choosing him over her."

How could anyone choose her dad over her mother? I couldn't picture that. My mother and I are so close, I couldn't imagine life without her. If seeing Dan Morris would make my mother feel that way, I definitely was not going to do it.

"It must be hard to have your father so far away,

Ashley," Nikki sympathized. Her real father was dead, and her mother had remarried a guy named Martin. That meant Nikki and her brother not only gained a stepfather, who Nikki adores, but they also got Eve in the bargain. The only problem is that Nikki's older stepsister is not Nikki's idea of a bargain.

To be honest, I like Eve. Nikki says that's because we're both super brains. Unfortunately, Nikki and Eve don't get along at all. I suppose it's harder to like people when you actually have to live with them.

"Why are you mad at Brittany Wells?" I asked Ashley, remembering the way she'd glared at Brittany.

"*She's* the one Kate thinks should interview for the California Essence job. And Brittany is just so sure she's going to get it. I hate her. She's so superior all the time," Ashley explained.

"How can you hate her?" Nikki asked. "She never says anything."

"I hate her, anyway," Ashley said, and pouted.

Just then the door creaked open, and in slipped our friend Chloe Chang. "Oh!" she cried, jumping back slightly. "I didn't expect to see you guys in here." She brushed the long black bangs of her stylish short haircut away from her almond-shaped eyes. "What's up?"

"Ashley's mad because Ms. Calico won't let her go out for some perfume ad," I told her.

"Not just *some* perfume ad!" cried Ashley. "It's a new line of stuff that's going to be pitched to teens. It's going to be really big! There will be TV commercials *and* print ads. But Kate thinks I'm too unsophisticated to sell perfume."

"That's crazy! You're the most sophisticated person I know," Chloe said, sitting down on the floor next to Ashley. Chloe and Ashley are best friends. They've been models since they were little kids. "I can't think of anyone more sophisticated than you," Chloe went on. "Well, maybe Brittany Wells is a touch more sophisticated, but . . ."

Ashley's glare stopped Chloe cold. "But maybe not," Chloe finished, switching gears quickly. "There's sophisticated and then there's *sophisticated*."

"What does that mean?" I asked irritably. I have no patience when people say stuff that doesn't mean anything.

"It means she realized she said the wrong thing," Ashley said with a half smile. "It's okay, Chloe. I'm just in a bad mood about this."

"Well, I'm in a bad mood, too," Chloe said. "I came in here to study. I have a big history test, and lately my dad has been on my case about schoolwork. I've been getting B's all along, but I got a little C on my last test and he went all zooey on me. He says if I have any C's on my report card, he'll cut down on my modeling schedule."

"My parents said that, too," said Nikki. "My mom isn't sure she likes the idea of me doing this, so I'm supposed to be on probation. If I get a bad report card this term, no modeling anymore, ever. I might not even be here now if Martin hadn't talked her into changing her mind and giving me a chance. Thank goodness for Martin. I can always count on him to help me out with Mom."

"My father is okay, I guess," Chloe conceded reluctantly. "It's just that he wants so much for my brothers and sisters and me that he pushes and pushes. I guess it's good that he cares, but he can be such a pain."

"You guys had better get good grades then," said Ashley.

While they grumbled about grades, my mind was on something else. Dads. Ashley was frantic to get this job so she could go to California to see her father. Nikki missed her dead dad but was crazy about her stepfather. Chloe's father was a pain in the neck, but you could tell they were tight. And what was I doing? Refusing to see my father. Yesterday it had seemed like the right thing to do. Suddenly I wasn't so sure.

At the same time, I didn't want Mom to feel bad. I was getting totally confused.

"Earth to Tracey." Nikki laughed. "What are you thinking? You look like you're a zillion miles away."

"I was thinking about fathers," I said. "Guess who called me yesterday? My long-lost father."

"No kidding!" Ashley gasped. "How great! When are you going to see him? Have you seen him already?"

"No," I said.

"Oh, then you'll have to find something good to wear," Ashley rambled on excitedly. "You want to make a good impression. I have the cutest jumper you could borrow. Dads like to see their daughters in dresses. It would look great on you, and I have shoes you could—"

"Hold on," I interrupted her. "I'm not going to see him."

"Why not?" Chloe cried.

I shrugged. "I've never met the guy."

"You must be pretty angry at him," Nikki observed.

"No," I said slowly. "I don't think so." But maybe I was. Although I'd thought I just didn't care about him, perhaps it was anger. "Do you mind if we don't talk about this anymore?" I asked my friends. All these new and confusing feelings were making me uncomfortable.

"Okay," Nikki agreed. "I have to go, anyway. I'm supposed to meet the photographer right now."

"Me, too," I said. "I have an interview with those cupcake dweebs."

"What are you guys doing afterward?" Chloe asked.

"Nothing," I said.

"Me, neither," said Nikki.

"Why don't you come down to my family's restaurant? You can have dinner," Chloe offered. "My mom makes great moo shu pork. It might cheer us all up."

We agreed to meet back at the Red Room when we were done with everything we had to do. Then I went to meet Renata Marco, Ms. Calico's assistant.

Renata is cool. She's in her thirties, but she looks younger. She's very petite and pretty and has this long, curly blond hair. She always wears gypsy-style clothes—gauzy skirts, shiny scarves, clunky jewelry, that sort of thing. Ashley says she's into things like astrology and palm reading, but I'm not sure what I think about that stuff.

"Hello, Tracey," said Renata, getting up from her desk when I came into her office. "Your new haircut looks super, by the way," she said. The agency had cut my shoulder-length brown hair into a blunt cut that came to my chin.

"Thanks," I replied.

We went into the conference room and met the advertising people in charge of the Dingaling Cupcake account. They were Ms. Cosgrove, a heavyset woman with short blond hair, and Mr. Nardone, a super skinny guy with big ears. The two of them looked like Jack Sprat and his wife.

"Good heavens, those eyes!" cried Ms. Cosgrove in a husky voice as she stared at my face. "We must have her! Must have her! She *is* the Dingaling Cupcake type. Absolutely. Stacey, you're perfect."

"Tracey," I corrected her.

"Of course," she said. "Can you be at our studio Monday afternoon at three o'clock?"

"I get out of school at one," I said, "but I have to get into the city. Could you make it three-thirty?"

Ms. Cosgrove looked at Mr. Nardone and he nodded. "Three-thirty it is!" she said. "See you Monday."

For the next hour, I sat in the Red Room and read a book for English class. I was up to a really scary part when suddenly Ashley and Chloe came in. "Aah!" I exclaimed, my heart pounding.

"Ready?" Ashley chirped brightly. "We're taking a cab downtown. Nikki will arrange everything with her stepsister and meet us there when her shoot is done."

When we got outside, it was really cold. Ashley darted into the street, waving her arm. A cab stopped, and she signaled for us to enter it.

"Brrr." Ashley shivered as we climbed inside. "I despise winter. I *have* to get to California." She told the driver the address of the Changs' restaurant, and soon we were fighting traffic going downtown.

Finally we got to Chloe's neighborhood. With a little imagination, you could pretend you were in China. The signs were all in Chinese and English, and most of the people on the busy narrow streets were Chinese.

The cab stopped in front of a corner restaurant with a sign that said CHANGS' GARDEN. Ashley paid the driver and we got out. "The restaurant isn't open yet, so we have to go in through the kitchen," Chloe explained.

We went around the corner, along an alley, and down some stairs that led to a door. As Chloe pushed open the door, I put on my sunglasses. I like to be prepared for the unknown.

The minute we stepped into the kitchen, I inhaled terrific smells.

I also feared for my life.

A tall Asian man in a chef's outfit was screaming in Chinese at the top of his lungs as he waved a large, glistening cleaver in the air!

Chapter Three

———◆———

Open the door very quietly," Chloe whispered as we slithered along the side wall of the kitchen. "Let's hope he doesn't notice us."

Our destination was a narrow door in the corner next to a large black stove. In the center of the kitchen, the big man was still yelling in Chinese. I wasn't sure who he was mad at, but three young men in white aprons stood together nervously as he ranted. His face was beet red with anger and his eyes were fiery. All in all, he made a very scary sight.

I was the first to reach the door. Unfortunately it creaked when I pulled it open. The three of us froze as the man whirled around toward us. "And what are you up to?" he roared.

For a moment, I thought he was talking to me, and my jaw dropped. Then I realized he was talking to Chloe.

"Hi, Dad," she said.

Dad? Poor Chloe!

"I was just going to put my stuff away, and then I thought maybe we could have something to eat," Chloe said quickly.

"Something to eat!" the man bellowed. "Perhaps if these three here did their work and the prep cook I hired showed up, we could all have something to eat. Maybe our customers could even have something to eat!"

"Do you need help?" Chloe asked.

"No, you have studying to do."

"I did it at the agency. I read for two hours in between appointments," Chloe told him. "And I read for two hours last night, too."

Mr. Chang peered at Chloe skeptically, as if trying to see from her expression if she was telling the truth. He must have decided she was. "I need help then," he said. "Tell your brothers and sister, too."

"Sure thing," said Chloe, prodding us through the door and up the stairs. "I'll be right down."

We hurried up the stairs and went through another door at the top. Behind that door was a big, open apartment. The living room was huge, and behind it was a slightly smaller dining room. "The dining room used to be the kitchen," Chloe explained as we took off our jackets. "But Dad had it ripped out. He said we didn't need a kitchen since we had a large one downstairs."

As she spoke, I could imagine Mr. Chang ripping the sink right out of the wall with his bare hands.

The living room and dining room didn't have a lot of furniture, but the few pieces there looked elegant. The dining room table was a shiny, deep reddish wood. The living room couch was low to the ground, with cushions of satiny blue and green stripes.

"This place is really gorgeous," I said sincerely.

"Thanks," said Chloe. "Come on to my room." We followed her down the hall to the last room. It was small, and the walls were full of pictures. The biggest one was a poster of the cute guys from "One Ashford Avenue."

Around the poster were ads torn from magazines. Some featured Ashley; others featured Chloe. Some of the ads went all the way back to when Ashley and Chloe were little girls. They were really cute kids, especially Chloe, who had worn her hair spiky and short.

Photos from the Cotton Kids photo shoot we'd done in Bermuda had just appeared in magazine ads, and Chloe had tacked them up, too. In one of them, Nikki was doing a cartwheel, her red hair flying all around her. They'd picked her to be the Cotton Kids spokesteen, along with a guy named Pablo Ruiz. It was a great deal for her, especially since she was just starting out.

"Sorry about my father, guys," Chloe said, shaking her head. "I have to go down and help. It won't take me more than an hour, tops."

"We can help you," Ashley offered.

Chloe looked uncertain. "It's not fun. It's a lot of chopping and washing and all."

"I don't mind," I said hesitantly, "but will your father throw a knife at me if I make a mistake?"

"Only if it seems like you're daydreaming," said Chloe, smiling. "He hates daydreaming."

"I just had a haircut," I said. "I don't need another."

"Don't worry," said Chloe. "He hasn't killed anybody yet."

"That's reassuring," I mumbled as we went back out into the hall.

Chloe pounded on each of the bedroom doors, calling to her brothers and sister as she moved along. "Dad wants help," she yelled after each knock. She didn't bother to wait for an answer. I guess with a father like that, nobody dared say no.

We headed into the kitchen. Chloe gave me a huge white apron, which I had to wrap around me twice, and a hair net. Ashley was given the same outfit and put to work taking the shells off about a billion pounds of shrimp. "It's so much nicer when they just hand you the shrimp cocktail," she said, wrinkling her nose in distaste as she sat on a stool and tossed shells into a paper bag.

I was set up with a knife and cutting board. Chloe gave me this fat, celery-like vegetable I'd never seen before. She said it was bok choy. All I had to do was slice it into thin pieces.

It seemed to me I was doing a great job as I chopped away. But then the large shadow of Mr. Chang loomed over me.

"No! No!" he thundered. "You are daydreaming!"

He took the knife from me and began chopping. His hands flew and so did the bok choy. I'd never seen anyone cut that fast. "There," he said, pointing to the pile of vegetable slices. "Like that." He grabbed my hand and curled my fingers under. "Keep your fingers wrapped around the knife like so. I don't want any fingertips in my bok choy. That makes the Department of Health very angry."

It was hard to tell if he was kidding. I figured he must be, but I wasn't sure enough to smile. "No problem," I said, taking the knife from him. I curled my fingers and started chopping away. Mr. Chang smiled down at me approvingly. "Good job!" he said when I was done. He patted my back so hard I went forward into the counter. "You can work for me anytime," he added.

I felt really proud of myself, as if I had just won a scholarship to Harvard or something. I picked up another piece of bok choy. Curling my fingers under again, I was determined to become the best chopper Mr. Chang had ever seen.

As I worked, Chloe's sister drifted in. She was tall and really beautiful, with silky black hair in a French braid. Her three brothers came down, too. The two older ones seemed like regular guys. One never took off his Walkman, and the other wore a football jersey. Chloe's younger brother, Tommy, was about nine. He wore his baseball cap backward and whistled while he chopped water chestnuts into slivers.

He'd obviously been instructed by the master.

A very old lady in a housedress entered the kitchen. Her gray hair was pulled back in a braid. She began seasoning the soup that simmered on the stove. Then Chloe's mother came in from outside, holding a paper bag of groceries in one arm and the cutest little girl you ever saw in the other. "What's all this?" she asked pleasantly.

"My prep cook never showed up," Mr. Chang informed her.

"Oh, dear," said Mrs. Chang, settling the girl on the floor and putting on an apron. The little girl was around two and she tottered around the kitchen, interested in everything that was going on.

I'd never met anyone with such a big family. As I looked around and watched everyone working, it seemed really great to me.

In a little over an hour, we got things together. Finally Mr. Chang told Ashley, Chloe, and me that he didn't need us anymore. He let Chloe's older sister, Michelle, leave, too. "Go memorize your bones," he said to her.

"Michelle is in her first year of med school," Chloe said as she led us into the empty restaurant. "The work is so hard she's in a state of shock."

The restaurant was simply decorated with white curtains and pretty watercolor landscapes hanging on the walls. Mrs. Chang came out behind us. "Thank you girls for your help," she said. "What can I get you to eat? You've earned a good meal."

"Thanks, Mom," said Chloe. "We're waiting for one more friend."

At that moment, Nikki rapped on the front door. Her breath made a little cloud of steam on the glass. Chloe took some keys from behind the cash register and opened it for her. "How was the shoot?" she asked when Nikki came in, flapping her arms for warmth.

"Cold!" Nikki said with a shiver. "But fun. Pablo is really nice."

"He's so quiet," observed Ashley.

"Yeah, but he has a funny sense of humor," Nikki said as she checked her watch. "We can stay only an hour and a half," she told me. "Eve said she'll pick us up promptly at six-thirty. And you know Eve."

"You could set your clock by her," I filled in.

"You should have invited her to come in and eat," said Chloe.

"You don't want Eve around, believe me," Nikki said, peeling off her denim jacket and then pulling off her heavy sweater. "She'd eat three plates of food and then advise you how to make it better, based on some public TV program she'd just seen."

When we were all seated, Mrs. Chang brought us the most delicious meal I've ever had in my life. We started with hot and sour soup. From the smell, I recognized it as the soup Chloe's grandmother had been seasoning. "This is Grandma's specialty," Chloe told us. "Nobody makes this soup like she does."

"Is she the grandmother who used to be a midwife in China?" Nikki asked. "The one who helped deliver you?"

"Yeah," said Chloe. "She's really cool."

"I wonder if my grandmother makes anything special," I blurted out.

My friends looked at me. "Don't you know?" Nikki asked.

"My father's mother, I mean," I explained. "I've never met her. I could ask Dan if his parents are alive, but then I'd have to see him, I guess."

"How strange not to know your grandmother," Chloe murmured softly.

"Maybe you should see him," Ashley suggested. "You could ask him about your grandmother and stuff like that."

I stirred my soup. "I don't know," I said, which was true. Yesterday I'd been so positive that I wanted no part of Dan Morris, but today I wasn't sure anymore.

After the soup, we had a plate of incredible spareribs. From there we went on to Mrs. Chang's famous moo shu pork, which we wrapped in steaming soft, thin pancakes. The gluey chow mein my mother heated up from a can was nothing like this. Not even close!

At six-thirty on the dot, Nikki's stepsister arrived to pick us up. Nikki and I were already standing outside the restaurant when Eve's clunky old car came banging up the street.

We climbed in and I saw a pile of books and tapes beside her. "What's that?" I asked.

"Books about learning Chinese," she said with a shake of her brownish blond hair. "And some audiocassettes to go with them." She'd spent the last hour poking around in some of the local shops. "Any Westerner who hopes to achieve anything on a global scale in the upcoming century will have to know one or more of the Asian languages," she announced in her superior way.

Nikki rolled her eyes, but this is the kind of thing that makes me like Eve, even though she *is* a tubby grouch. She's interesting. When she's not eating or complaining, she comes out with stuff that makes you think.

Eve dropped me off in front of Paradise Gardens, and I walked through the courtyard toward my building. The light near my stairway had been out for about a week, so it was always a little creepy at night. I usually just started running while I was still near the streetlight and raced through the darkest part until I was at my door.

I was preparing to run, when I heard a noise by the stairs. I looked hard into the darkness and saw the dim outline of a person.

Then the man stepped out of the shadows and I saw his face. Although he was a stranger, I knew who he was.

"Tracey?" he said.

Speechless, I nodded.

"Hi. I'm your father."

Chapter Four

———◆———

Pretty snazzy place, huh?" said Dan Morris as he sat across the table from me at Clancy's Steakhouse.

"Snazzy?" I asked, adjusting my sunglasses nervously.

He laughed, and his aqua blue eyes twinkled. "Snazzy is an old-time term. It's even older than my generation. My dad used to say it. It means fancy, nice."

"Yeah, it is cool—snazzy," I agreed. I'd always wanted to go to Clancy's. Mom said it was too expensive. But it always looked so nice to me when we drove by—all warm and cozy, with flickering lights that you could see through the big front window. Now I saw that the flickering was coming from a stone fireplace along the wall. Dan and I were at a table not far from it.

"Can I ask you a personal question, Tracey?"

"I suppose."

"What's with the shades? Is something wrong with your eyes?"

"No, I just like to wear them," I said. I'd put them on as soon as I'd gotten into the car with him. I always feel less nervous wearing them.

"That's better," he said with an approving nod as I slipped the glasses off. "You've got the Morris eyes. Our trademark."

I now knew where I got my eyes from. In fact, I knew where I'd got my entire self from. I looked just like Dan Morris.

The waitress came to take our order. She was wearing an old-fashioned dress with a ruffled apron. Her badge had "Suzie" on it. Dan looked up and smiled at her. "Hi there, Suzie. That's one of my favorite names. I have a sister named Suzie."

Suzie smiled. "Thanks."

"I'll just have a shrimp cocktail," I said, still full from my Chinese feast.

"Come on, Tracey," Dan encouraged me. "Pig out!"

"I can't, really," I protested. But everything smelled so good. "I'll have an order of cheddar-and-bacon potato skins, too," I added. I can never resist those.

"That's the girl!" said Dan. Then he ordered a big steak, baked potato, and a salad.

"Anything to drink?" Suzie asked.

Suddenly I froze, remembering what my mother had said about him being a drunken idiot.

What had I gotten myself into? I'd agreed to go to dinner with him because for some reason I didn't want to bring him into the apartment. I wasn't sure how Mom would react, and I wasn't sure I wanted him in my house, either. What if he got drunk now? What if he made a scene, or wanted to drive me home drunk?

"A Coke," he said. "How about you, Tracey?"

"Coke, too," I ordered with a smile. Whew!

I guess my worries showed all over my face. Dan put his big hand over mine. "I've been off the booze for a year now," he said. "I suppose your mom has told you what a drunken jerk I used to be?"

"She uses the word *idiot*," I told him bluntly as I slid my hand away.

"Yeah, that, too," he agreed. "But I'm in Alcoholics Anonymous. It's a group that helps you stop drinking and stay off it. Part of what they ask you to do is make amends to people you've hurt because of your drinking. Of all the people I've hurt, I've probably hurt you the most."

"You haven't hurt me," I quickly disagreed. "How can a person you've never seen before hurt you?"

"I hurt you a lot simply by not being there for you," he insisted.

I started fiddling with my napkin. "It doesn't matter. We're doing all right without you."

"Every kid deserves a dad," he said.

Luckily Suzie arrived with the sodas. This conversation was making me uncomfortable. I didn't feel like I needed a dad. At least, I never had before. But here was something weird: I liked Dan Morris. Though I hadn't wanted to like him, it was hard not to.

When our food came, we ate without talking much. Now I knew where my huge appetite came from. He didn't leave a crumb on his plate.

After we were done and Suzie cleared our plates, he took out his wallet. "This is my wife, Janine," he said, opening to a bunch of pictures covered in plastic. He took a picture out of its holder and handed it to me. A woman with long strawberry blond hair stood in front of a simple, but nice, house. "That's our home in Arizona."

Beside Janine was a collie. "This your dog?" I asked.

"Yeah, that's Gale. We found her in a storm, so we named her that."

"Cool," I said, thinking of the dog I'd found last night. I'd slept with him all night. In the morning, I'd left him in my room with a bowl of water and some Cheerios. I hoped he'd be all right until I got home.

"Janine is here with me," Dan went on. "Maybe you'll get a chance to meet her."

"Maybe," I said. I wasn't sure, though. Did that mean I was going to see Dan again? Everything seemed so up in the air right now.

Outside, there was a flash of lightning and a bang of thunder. Then a cloud just seemed to open up right over Clancy's. Buckets of rain came pouring down the big window. The drops made a racket on the roof. "Wow!"

Dan said. "Pretty dramatic weather."

"Yeah." I laughed. "If there's anything I hate, it's boring weather."

"Me, too," Dan said, smiling. "Like father, like daughter. I love rainstorms."

So did I, but somehow I didn't feel like saying so. It was too soon to think of myself as his daughter, and as being like him. For now, he was just Dan, this guy who had suddenly popped up out of nowhere. That was all.

"I'd better call Mom," I said. "She doesn't know where I am. She'll be expecting me home by now."

"Sure, call," Dan agreed.

I found the pay phone, but nobody picked up. I wish we had an answering machine. My mother doesn't want one, though. She says that if we don't have a machine, people from work can't bug her as much.

"Well, I guess she's not worried," I said when I returned to the table. "She's not even home. Maybe she went out with Mel again."

"Who is Mel?" Dan asked.

"Some guy she's started dating. I don't know him too well yet."

Dan and I split a piece of blueberry pie, and then he paid the check. I peeked at the total while he went to the men's room. It was a whopper! My mother had been right.

On the ride home, he told me he was a computer repairman. "That sounds pretty interesting," I said. I think everything about computers is fascinating.

"It is," he said as we stopped at a traffic signal. The red light shone on his face through the wet windshield. He was pretty handsome in a middle-aged kind of way. "How are you doing in school?" he asked.

"No sweat," I told him. "I'm in all advanced classes. And I've already taken so many of my required courses that I can get out of school at one o'clock for modeling."

He looked at me, his eyes wide. "I knew it. You're Maureen all over again."

"Who?"

"Maureen, my sister, your aunt. She's a super brain, the smartest in our family," Dan said as he pulled in front of Paradise Gardens.

"Do I have any other aunts and uncles?" I asked.

"Oh, sure," he said with a smile. "Hasn't your mother ever told you about them?"

"No," I answered. "I think she'd rather forget about you, and I suppose that means forgetting about the rest of your family, too."

A guilty look came across Dan's face. "I shouldn't blame your mother for something that's my fault. But, listen, I'm more together now. For the first time, I have some money. I'll start sending some to your mother. It's only right."

"Okay," I said, not knowing what else to say.

Then there was a long silence. Our conversation seemed to have run out of steam. "Well, so long," I said, feeling kind of awkward. "It was nice to meet you."

Dan unbuckled his seat belt. "I'll walk you. That

courtyard is pretty dark."

"Okay," I agreed. He pulled a large black umbrella from the backseat just as another thunderclap sounded. He got out on his side and ran around to me, holding the umbrella over my head as I climbed out of the car.

As we walked through the dark courtyard, I couldn't help thinking it was nice to have someone holding an umbrella over my head, someone big who made me stop worrying about shadows. I'd thought I didn't need a dad, but maybe I'd just never known what I was missing.

We were walking up the stairs when I saw a woman come running across the courtyard. As she came into the light, I saw that it was my mother.

Her thin raincoat was pulled tightly around her, and her wet hair was plastered to her head. "Tracey!" she screamed from halfway across the courtyard. "Where on earth have you been?"

As she got closer, I saw that the rain had smeared her mascara under her eyes. When she caught sight of Dan, she looked like a startled raccoon.

"I tried to call, but no one was home," I defended myself.

"I was out looking for you," she said. Her voice had quieted down to a shocked murmur. She just kept staring at Dan as if he were a ghost. "When did you get here?" she asked him coldly.

"Yesterday," he said. "I tried to call you, Caroline, but no one was home and I don't have your work number."

My mother kept coming toward us, her eyes darting between Dan and me. "You should have waited until you spoke to me," she told Dan. "And you, Tracey, should have left me a note. I came home and heard something in your room. For an entire hour, I assumed you were home. Then I heard whimpering and opened the door. Instead of you, there was a . . . a . . . a dog in your room!"

"I meant to tell you about him," I said.

"That would have been nice," my mother said angrily. "That little dog could have gotten us thrown out of the apartment. If someone reports us, we could be evicted."

"You didn't put him out, did you?" I asked.

"Of course I did."

"Mom!" I shouted. "Now he's out in this storm! How could you be so mean?"

"How could you be so thoughtless?" Mom shouted back. "You know the rules."

"Maybe I'd better go," Dan said.

Mom whirled around to him angrily. "Yes, maybe you had better!"

He hurried down the stairs and across the courtyard. As I closed the apartment door behind me, I took another look at him. A flash of lightning lit his broad-shouldered back as he disappeared into the darkness.

Chapter Five

———◄•►———

You know the deal, right, Tracey?" said Eve on Monday after school as we stood in front of her house. Nikki was there, too, raking leaves. She didn't have a modeling job that day, but I did. My big Dingaling debut.

"Right," I said. "I pay for a tank of gas, all the tolls, and a parking garage if you need one." Eve had a study hall at the end of the day, so she got out of school early enough to drive Nikki and me into the city when we had modeling jobs. Originally Eve had started taking Nikki into the city just as an excuse to drive. Soon she started bargaining for gas, then tolls. The garage thing was her latest money-maker. I suspected that she skimmed a few dollars off the top of the garage price.

Nikki's stepdad, Martin, appeared at the front door and called to Eve. He looked like a typical dad, right out of a television show—slightly bald, slightly paunchy. He was even wearing a brown cardigan sweater with suede patches on the elbows. Total dadness.

"What a pain! What does he want now?" Eve sighed. "He's not even supposed to be home today."

"Martin came home to work on a legal case," Nikki explained to me. "He says he can concentrate better at home without all the phones ringing."

"But all he does is drive us crazy with his nagging," Eve grumbled as she headed off across the lawn. The funny thing is that Nikki gets along great with Martin, but Eve and he are always at odds.

"Don't take long," I called to Eve. "I have to be there by three-thirty."

While I waited for Eve, I told Nikki about my pal, the stray dog. I'd found him again on Sunday morning. He was all wet and whimpery, but when I opened the front door to get the newspaper, there he was, waiting for me. I didn't want to get my mother all shaken up again, so I went back and got him a bowl of Cheerios and fed him on the porch. While he ate, I toweled him dry. I decided to call him Tuffy, since he seemed to be such a tough little guy, surviving out on his own like that.

"So, do you think you'll see your dad again?" Nikki asked. Yesterday I'd called and told her everything that had happened with Dan Morris.

"No," I said. "And don't call him my dad, okay?"

"Why not?" Nikki asked.

"I don't know. It just sounds too strange."

"All right," she agreed. "Tell me why you aren't going to see *Mr. Morris* again. Do you know where to reach him?"

"Yeah. He called later on Sunday, and I spoke to him after he talked to my mother for a while. Whatever he said to her cooled her down. He wanted to see me again, but I said no. Meeting him was okay. I mean, he was pretty nice and all. But I don't want to see him again."

"Why not?" Nikki asked as she raked.

I shrugged. "What's the point?" I figured, why get all involved with someone who was just going to disappear back to Arizona.

"You're strange," Nikki said, shaking her head.

At that moment, Eve came back out of the house and waved for me to get into her car, which was parked in the driveway. "So long," I told Nikki as I ran over.

Traveling with Eve is a really wild experience since she drives like a complete maniac. She cuts people off, screams out the window at anyone who annoys her—which is everyone—and is not a bit shy about leaning on her horn. But her driving did get us into the city quickly. In twenty-five minutes, we pulled up in front of a fancy-looking building, all glittering chrome and glass, on a busy main street. Eve said she'd call in two hours to find out when to meet me.

Inside the building, a doorman in a military-type uniform walked up to me. "May I help you?" he asked in a very superior voice.

"I have an appointment at the office of Cubb, Slubberton, and Boynton," I said, imitating his superior tone.

He directed me to the fifteenth floor, where I asked the receptionist for Ms. Cosgrove. In a few minutes, she appeared, all bouncy and perky. "Stacey!" she cried, holding out her arms.

I didn't know if she expected me to hug her, but I certainly wasn't going to. "Hi," I said. "It's Tracey. Tracey Morris."

"Yes, of course. Come with me." She took me down a bunch of long halls to a big open room with a kitchen in it. "We're going to use our in-house studio today rather than go all the way to a photographer's studio."

I noticed that the counter of the kitchen was loaded high with cellophane-wrapped packages of Dingaling cupcakes, only they weren't brown like the usual chocolate ones. These were an unnatural bright orange.

"This ad will be for the new line of pumpkin cupcakes. The Dingaling people are rushing them onto the market," Ms. Cosgrove told me.

Just then, a blond woman dressed in a mannish business suit strode into the middle of the room. "Tell me this isn't the model," she said to Ms. Cosgrove in a loud, forceful voice.

"Yes, this is Stacey—"

"Tracey," I said.

"She's no good," said the woman. "We wanted a blond kid. I specifically told you a blond kid. The other kid was a blonde. What happened to her?"

"This is Muffy Addams of the Dingaling Company," Ms. Cosgrove told me. "Not to worry, Muffy. We have things under control." Ms. Cosgrove opened a cabinet and pulled out a curly blond wig on a white Styrofoam head.

"Take this wig to Theresa over there," Ms. Cosgrove said, pointing to a dark-haired young woman in a skin-tight dress. She stood, chewing gum and looking bored, in front of a swivel chair and a mirror.

I brought her the wig and climbed into the chair. Theresa looked at the wig and made a disgusted face. "They really want me to put this mop on your head?" she asked me.

"They want a blond model," I told her.

"Do they want a girl or a poodle?" Theresa asked, snapping her gum.

"A poodle-ish girl, I guess," I said.

That made Theresa laugh. "Ha! You're a scream, kid. Take off the dark goggles and let's get this thing over with."

As I took off my sunglasses, she pinned back my dark hair and then tugged the blond wig into place. "It looks horrible," I said.

"I know," Theresa agreed. "Even though you have those crazy blue eyes, you have dark eyebrows. Blond hair is all wrong for your coloring."

Ms. Cosgrove didn't agree. "Fabulous!" she pronounced, clapping her hands gleefully. "You see, Muffy, problem fixed."

51

Muffy walked around me in a circle. "Good enough," she muttered. "She'll simply have to do. We're late enough as it is."

Muffy didn't exactly make me feel great. Certainly not *fabulous*.

"Get some makeup on her," Ms. Cosgrove told Theresa. "She's so pale, the lights will wash out her face completely."

Theresa began smearing makeup on my face with a damp sponge. It felt gross. Then she put pink lip gloss on me, and so much mascara that my lashes felt as if the tops and bottoms were going to stick together.

When Theresa was done, Ms. Cosgrove came over holding a dress on a hanger. "You'll wear this," she said. "Isn't it adorable?"

"A little too adorable," I said, horrified. The dress was a red checked thing with puffed sleeves. "Do I have to?" I asked.

"I'm afraid so," Ms. Cosgrove said. "Muffy picked it out herself."

"It figures," I mumbled as I took the dress and went behind a screen to change. When I came out, I walked past the mirror.

Big mistake.

I looked like I was dressed as some kind of demented oversize doll for Halloween.

"Fabulous, Stacey, fabulous," said Ms. Cosgrove, whisking me over to meet a photographer named Neil, a short guy in a flannel Hawaiian print shirt.

"Okay, Stacey," he said. "Just munch down on a cupcake and we'll have you out of here in a jiff."

"No problem," I said.

Muffy Addams put her hands on my shoulders and pushed me along to the cabinet. "Here's the idea," she said. "You can't wait for dinner. You have to have your Dingaling pumpkin cupcakes *now*! Can you do that?"

"Sounds easy," I replied.

"Well, it shouldn't!" Muffy snapped. "We need to see passion for that cupcake. You have to really crave it with everything inside you. You can't be casual about a Dingaling cupcake."

"She can do it, Muffy," said Ms. Cosgrove. "That's why we selected her. She has passion-for-cupcakes written all over her face."

I did? I made a mental note to be more careful about that in the future.

They had me pull open the cabinet door and bite into a pumpkin cupcake. Pulling open the door was no problem. Biting the cupcake was another story.

Yuck!

Chocolate Dingalings are great, but these pumpkin things were disgusting. "What's the problem? What's the problem?" Muffy screamed.

"It's these cupcakes," I said. "They're so—"

"Incredibly delicious," Ms. Cosgrove jumped in. "But we're not seeing that, Stacey. I know you're thinking it—we're just not seeing it in your face. We need much more delight."

"All right," I agreed. "And it's Tracey. My name is Tracey."

"Of course it is," said Ms. Cosgrove as she handed me another cupcake. "Try it again. And remember, it's fabulous!"

I tried. I really did. I bit the cupcake and tried to look delighted. But let me tell you, that's not easy to do when you want to throw up. The cupcakes were extremely sweet, yet they tasted so pumpkiny I couldn't stand them. "What's this crunchy stuff in them?" I asked, after about the fifteenth unsuccessful cupcake bite.

"Dehydrated carrot bits," Muffy said proudly. "We want health-conscious parents to approve."

Dried carrot bits! I wished I hadn't asked. "Try again," said Ms. Cosgrove, handing me another disgusting cupcake.

For the sixteenth time, I pulled open the cabinet door. The bobby pins Theresa had used to keep the wig in place were sticking into my scalp. The elastics on the puffed sleeves were cutting into my arms. The hot lights were turning the makeup on my skin into goo. And the thought of biting into one more cupcake made my stomach flip-flop.

But I did it. You love this cupcake, I told myself as I sank my teeth into it.

Click. "This is the one," Neil said, snapping his camera.

Yes! I thought hopefully. I've done it!

"I think that's the one," said Ms. Cosgrove happily. "That looked good to me."

I put down the cupcake and heaved a sigh of relief.

54

"No!" Muffy screeched, charging over to me. "What is the matter with you people? That was terrible! This girl isn't wild for Dingaling pumpkin cupcakes. Any idiot could see that." She wheeled around and stuck her face into mine. "What kind of model are you? Don't you know how to do your job?"

"I don't know how to pretend I love these revolting cupcakes!" I yelled back at her. I took the cupcake in my hand and smashed it icing-down on the counter. Then I clawed at the stupid wig until it was off my head. "Find yourself another Dingaling girl. I quit!"

This might have been a great and dramatic moment, except for one thing. As I stormed toward the door, I ran smack into the most intimidating person I've ever met.

Kate Calico, head of the Calico Modeling Agency!

Chapter Six

———◆———

Yes, Ms. Calico," I mumbled. "I realize modeling is hard work. I know it's not just glamour and high pay."

Ms. Calico sat on a folding chair in the corner of the studio. On the outside, Ms. Calico is not particularly terrifying. In fact, she's very beautiful. She has short brown hair, big brown eyes, and a perfect figure, and always wears terrific suits.

But she made me nervous from the first minute I met her. Ms. Calico would be the ideal school principal or even president of the United States. The minute you see her, you know she's totally confident, and totally the boss. She has a lovely, silky voice and never yells. Still, I've seen her fix an expression on people that made them incapable of going against her.

I was locked in the grip of that expression as we spoke.

"Tracey, listen to me," Ms. Calico said in her smooth voice. "Muffy Addams is a fool. Everyone in the industry knows it except for Muffy. Someone who knows what she's doing doesn't have to rant and scream like that. It's a sign of her weakness, not her strength."

I never would have thought of it that way, but it made sense. Still, there was only so much a person could put up with. "Did you hear the way she was talking to me?" I protested.

"Yes. It was unacceptable."

"So, what was I supposed to do?"

Ms. Calico frowned. "As long as you are a Calico model, you get the job done. No matter what, the job is completed professionally."

"That means no quitting," I said, getting her meaning.

"Not unless the situation is dangerous to you."

"Eating those cupcakes could be dangerous," I muttered.

Ms. Calico smiled. "Come with me," she said, taking my wrist as she stood up. She drew me over to Muffy Addams. "Hello, Muffy," Ms. Calico said pleasantly.

"Oh, Kate, hello," Muffy said. "Have you been able to talk some sense into that kid?"

"No, Muffy, it's *you* I've come to talk to."

"Me?" Muffy snapped. "I'm doing all I can to make this ad work. We are behind schedule and—"

"Have you tasted the product?" Ms. Calico pressed.

"Not personally, but I've been assured it's a wonderful

cupcake, sure to—"

While Muffy was talking, Ms. Calico unwrapped a cupcake and handed it to her. "Try one," she suggested.

Everyone watched Muffy Addams bite into a Dingaling pumpkin cupcake. It was hard not to burst out laughing. Her eyes widened and her nostrils flared as she tasted it. "Not bad," she mumbled through tightly closed lips, without swallowing the cupcake. Her expression was so sour, it was easy to tell what she really thought. "It's a new taste sensation that might take some getting used to."

"Here's a suggestion," Ms. Calico said pleasantly. "Why not have Tracey looking at the cupcake? It is a pretty-looking thing, isn't it, Tracey?"

"It is," I admitted cooperatively.

Ms. Calico put her arm around me. "You could pretend you were sneaking a snack before supper. The greatest snack ever made."

"All right," I said, holding up the blond wig. "I'll have to go put this thing on first."

"Muffy," Ms. Calico said, "Tracey's own hair is so lovely. And that wig and dress make her look like a little girl. It seems to me that preteens and teens have more money to spend on snacks than children do. And perhaps children aren't quite ready for this type of cupcake. You might do better trying to sell it to an older child, someone more Tracey's age."

"Skip the wig," Muffy commanded. "And the dress.

Let's just get this thing shot."

"Change into your own clothes and brush your hair," Ms. Calico told me. "Wipe some of that heavy makeup off, too."

Thanks to Ms. Calico, the shoot was done in less than fifteen minutes. I looked adoringly at the cupcake. Neil took a bunch of pictures while I changed the position of my head and hands slightly for each shot. And then it was over.

"Nice work," said Ms. Calico as I gathered my things to leave. She opened her small purse and handed me a cream-colored envelope. "It's an invitation to my annual holiday party," she explained. "All the Calico models are invited. I do hope you can come. Bring your family. It's a big party."

"Thank you," I said, taking the invitation from her. "And thank you for your help."

"You're most welcome, Tracey," she said. "You have lots of spirit. Use it correctly and you will be a great model. Let it get the better of you, and it will always be a problem. Tantrums can end a modeling career."

"I understand," I said.

The receptionist called me over as I passed her desk. "Are you the model from Calico?" she asked. "Somebody named Eve left you this phone number. She said to call when you were ready to be picked up."

"Thanks," I said, taking a slip of paper with the number from her.

I stared down at the phone number and decided not to call right away. Despite Ms. Calico's help, I was in a terrible mood and needed time to cool down. I pulled on my coat and went out to the elevator. I decided that a walk around the block might help.

There was so much I wanted to think about. I had never really made up my mind whether or not I wanted to be a model. So far, it had just been for fun. Even Bermuda had been fun—modeling in a group and being in such a great place. This was my first taste of the hard-work part of modeling. It was also my first experience with someone like Muffy Addams. I wasn't so sure I wanted any part of it.

When the elevator door opened, I jumped back in surprise.

Dan Morris was in the elevator.

"What are you doing here?" I gasped.

"I was coming up to leave a note for you," he said with a smile. "I called your mother this morning, and she told me you'd be here. Don't worry, it's okay with her. I told her I was going to ask you about spending some time together this evening. She said it was up to you. All she asks is that you call her and tell her what you've decided to do. Janine is waiting in the car. Want to meet her?"

"I suppose," I said, shrugging.

"I asked your mother how she felt about my showing up," Dan said as we went down in the elevator together. "She said she thought it was good for you and me to get to know each other. I was glad to hear that."

"Mom's cool," I said. "She comes off like a flake, but she's pretty tough."

"I know," he said, and there was a lot of sadness in his voice. "I guess she's had to be tough."

Dan's car was parked at a bus stop in front of the building. In the passenger seat sat a pretty woman with lots of long red hair. "Hurry up there, Dan," she said with a heavy western twang. "One of those big old city buses is heading right for us."

I climbed into the backseat as Dan hopped into the front. We pulled out just as a bus pulled in. "Hi, Tracey," said Janine, turning around in her seat. She looked like a cowgirl in a denim shirt, jeans, and boots. "I've heard so much about you. I suppose you didn't expect to get hijacked today, did you?"

"No, but it's okay," I said. The truth was that seeing Dan and now Janine had lifted my spirits. I wasn't sure why.

"I got tickets for a play," Dan told me. "Would you like to see the revival of *Singing in the Rain?*"

"Sure," I said. "The only plays I've ever seen have been school plays."

"You're in for a treat," said Dan. "First you'd better call your mother."

"And Eve. She's my ride home," I added. Dan stopped at a phone booth. I called Eve and then I called my mother. "I'm with Dan," I told Mom. "He's taking me to a play."

"How nice," she said, but her voice was sad. "Mel and I are going out for supper. Maybe you'll join us next time."

"Sure," I said. Now I felt sad, too. My mother and I almost always have supper together. Maybe it was just the change in routine that bothered us.

As I hung up the phone, a cold wind ran up my back. I shivered and held myself tight for warmth. Over at the curb, Dan and Janine sat inside the car with the heater on, laughing and listening to the radio while they waited for me. They looked so happy, and the car seemed so warm and inviting that I couldn't wait to get back inside.

We drove way uptown to a small German restaurant on a crowded street. After we stuffed ourselves, we went to the play. It was the most exciting thing! When the main character did his big dance in the rain, there was actual water pouring onto the stage. I got slightly splashed when he stomped around in it.

On the way home, we were all pretty tired, full, and quiet. Dan asked Janine if she was all right. "I was just thinking about Gale," she said. "I hope she's okay. My sister will look in on her every day, but she's never been left alone before."

"She'll be fine," said Dan. "You treat that dog like a baby. You should see, Tracey. She has a luxury heated doghouse, but she sleeps in our bed, anyway."

"I know I go a little overboard," Janine said with a smile. "I can't help worrying, though. Do you have a dog, Tracey?"

"Not really," I replied. "I mean, I feed a stray who comes around. I call him Tuffy. But we can't have pets in the apartment."

"Tuffy—that's cute," Janine said. "Too bad you can't keep him."

"Yeah," I agreed.

They drove me to the apartment, and I said good-bye to Janine in the car. Dan walked me across the courtyard and through the dreaded dark shadow. "I'll wait to see that you get in okay," he said as he stood on the porch with his hands jammed into the pockets of his coat. I used my key and went inside. The apartment was dark. When I turned on the light, I saw a note on the table: *At Burgerland with Mel. Love, Mom.*

I went back outside to say good-bye to Dan. "Mom will be home soon," I told him. "Thanks for everything. I had a great time."

"Thanks for coming out," he said. "It's great having a daughter. Especially a terrific one like you."

Something told me to say something nice back and hug him. That's what would have happened on a television show. But I couldn't.

"Well, I'll call you tomorrow," Dan said, backing away.

"All right. Thanks again." I stood there and watched him make his way through the courtyard. When I looked down, there was Tuffy, his little pink tongue sticking out of his mouth. "Hey, guy," I said, scooping him up. He was cold and shivered when I touched him.

"Too bad we're not in Arizona," I said as I petted him. "I know of this great heated doghouse nobody is using." I'm not sure why, but the thought of Tuffy in that empty doghouse, all safe and warm, made me start crying.

Chapter Seven

The rest of the week was pretty quiet. I didn't have any bookings with the agency, so I didn't have to go into the city. I saw Dan and Janine one night for a movie and pizza, which was fun.

My mother was out with Mel a lot. But one night, they just hung around the house and had pizza and played cards. I didn't have anywhere to go, and the smell of the pizza brought me out of my room. "Here she is," Mel said in his usual serious tone. "How's the studying going?"

"I'm not studying," I said as I pulled a slice out of the pie.

"What are you up to in there?" he asked.

The truth was that I was playing with Tuffy, but of course I couldn't say that, since Tuffy wasn't even supposed to be in the apartment at all. "Nothing," I said.

"You were just sitting in your room doing nothing?" he

questioned, as if it were any of his business.

"Yeah," I said, feeling myself getting annoyed.

"Do you often sit around and do nothing?" he asked. He just didn't give up!

"Oh, I'm sure Tracey was doing something," Mom said, a nervous cheeriness in her voice. "You were probably reading, weren't you, honey? Tracey reads all the time."

"No, I wasn't. I was doing nothing," I insisted. Now I was being a brat, but I couldn't seem to stop myself.

"That can be a sign of depression," Mel said. "Is anything bothering you, Tracey?"

Yeah, you! That's what I felt like saying, but for Mom's sake, I didn't. "Nothing is bothering me," I said, turning away, pizza in hand. "Now if you'll excuse me, I'll return to my pursuit of nothingness."

Feeling very dramatic, I waltzed off to my room. "She seems troubled," I heard Mel say as I closed the door.

Troubled! What nerve! Some counselor. He couldn't even tell when someone was goofing on him. I couldn't figure out how Mom could stand him.

Most of the time, thank goodness, Mom and Mel went out to a movie or something. That meant I was able to take Tuffy out into the living room. Before they got home, I put him back into my room to sleep. But one morning he slipped out of my room and woke my mother a full hour before she had to get up for work. Needless to say, she wasn't too pleased with either of us.

One afternoon I got home from school late because I

had a meeting. Mom was there, and one look at her face told me something was wrong.

"What's up?" I asked.

She held out a cream-colored card. I recognized it immediately. It was the invitation to Kate Calico's holiday party. "I went into your room to get a hairbrush and found this on the floor."

I shrugged off my jacket and took the invitation from her. "Oh, yeah, I forgot about this." That wasn't entirely true. Everyone at the agency was excited about the party. Ashley, Chloe, and Nikki were going crazy trying to decide what to wear.

"It says to Tracey Morris and family," my mother pointed out unnecessarily. "Is there some reason you didn't tell me about it?"

My heart did a quick flip-flop. Until that second, I had pushed the party out of my mind. Now I realized why. I didn't want to deal with the "and family" part.

Who was my family, anyway? Mom, of course. But Mom would want to bring Mel. I wasn't ready to introduce Mel to my friends as a member of my family. What about Dan? I wasn't exactly ready to accept him as a member of the family, either. And then there was Janine. She was fine, but I couldn't exactly walk in there with this whole crowd and say, "Hi, all these people are my parents."

Or could I? Lots of kids at school had two sets of parents. I suppose it wasn't all that bizarre. But they knew their parents. The only one I knew very well was Mom!

"Tracey, you're not answering me," Mom coaxed gently. "Were you going to tell me about this party?"

"I told you, I forgot about it," I insisted. "If you want to go, we can go."

"It sounds nice. Would you mind if I invited Mel?"

I knew it! "If you don't tell anyone he's my father."

"Of course I wouldn't!" Mom said firmly. Then her voice softened. "Don't you like Mel?"

"He makes me feel like I'm always in the guidance counselor's office. He's always asking me questions about myself and how I feel about things. Why doesn't he just talk to me like a regular person?"

"That's Mel's way. He's been a counselor for so long— that's how he's used to approaching new people. He only wants to get to know you."

"Well, he bugs me. Maybe it's just that I don't know him too well."

"Tracey, we'd do more things together, but you've been so busy lately between your school, your modeling, and . . . and . . . your . . . Dan Morris."

"Dan and Janine are fun," I said defensively.

"Yes, I can tell you like him," my mother said. "You know, he's going to return to Arizona. I worry that you might get too attached to him."

"Why shouldn't I get attached to him?" I heard myself ask. I couldn't believe how angry and defensive I sounded.

"Dan was always . . . unreliable," Mom said slowly. "Though since he's no longer drinking, that may have changed. Still, I would hate to see you get hurt."

"I won't get hurt," I said angrily.

"Mel isn't like Dan," Mom continued. "He's someone you can count on."

"*You* count on him then. I don't need him!"

The words came out of my mouth and seemed to hang in the air between us. I wanted to hide from the words, to hide from my mother—to hide from the whole world. As hot tears sprang to my eyes, I ran to my room.

Grabbing my pillow, I sat at the end of the bed and buried my face in it. How had this happened? How had I grown so close to Dan in such a short time? I hadn't wanted to, but I'd come to think of him as my dad. He *was* my dad, for heaven's sake! But I didn't want to love him.

I didn't want him to leave me again, because this time I would know what was happening. This time, it would really, *really* hurt.

The phone rang in the living room. When Mom didn't pick it up, I went out to answer it. The front door was ajar. I saw Mom standing outside on the porch, looking at the courtyard. "Hello," I said into the phone.

It was Ashley. "Hi," she began breathlessly. "I called to ask what you're wearing to the party, because I was looking through a catalog and I just saw this totally adorable green dress. But Chloe has a green dress and Nikki is thinking about buying a green-and-blue dress, so I figured that if you were going to wear green, too, then I couldn't buy this dress. Don't you think it would look weird? I mean, we don't want to look like escapees from the Emerald City or anything."

"I'm not wearing anything to the party," I said.

"What?" Ashley cried in alarm.

"I mean I'm not going to the party."

"You're not *what?*" she shrieked. This apparently shocked her even more than the idea of my showing up with no clothes on. "You have to go! First of all, it's a blast. Second of all, you have to see Kate's house. It's beyond belief. Third, you meet everybody at the agency. My mother always says it doesn't hurt to know people when you're in show business."

"We're not in show business," I pointed out.

"Oh, we practically are," Ashley disagreed. "It's almost the same thing."

"Well, I still don't think I want to go."

"It won't be as much fun without you," Ashley said.

That got to me. Ashley and I couldn't have been more different. She came from big bucks and I came from practically no bucks. And Ashley was super feminine and had been a model forever, while I could barely stand a dress and wasn't sure even now about modeling. Still, I liked Ashley—she had guts and she was a fighter. I was glad she liked me.

"I'd come, I guess, but it's a family issue," I told her. Then I explained how I felt. "It's like displaying my whole messed-up family in front of everyone," I said.

There was silence on the other end. "I'm shocked," she said at last.

"I know, my family is pretty weird," I agreed.

"No, I'm shocked that you think your family is weird," Ashley said. "Where have you been? In a cave?"

"What do you mean?" I asked.

"I mean everyone has a messed-up family nowadays. Well, practically everyone. Chloe and Nikki don't. But a lot of people do. Your family can't be weirder than mine. It's all how you look at it."

"I suppose," I said.

"Suppose, nothing!" she cried. "Just bring them all. No one will even notice. Everyone there will be too busy trying to get on Kate's good side to notice anything."

Ashley sure made it sound simple. In fact, she made me feel pretty silly for even worrying about it. "So you think I should invite Dan and Janine and Mom and Mel?" I asked.

"Why not?"

"All right," I agreed. "I think I've hurt Mom's feelings by not telling her about the party. She thinks I'm ashamed of her, or I don't like Mel, or I'd prefer to go with Dan."

"Then you have to tell her you want her to come," Ashley said.

"I will," I said. "I'm glad you called."

"Me, too," said Ashley. "There's only one more thing I have to tell you."

"What?"

"Don't you dare wear green!"

Chapter Eight

———— ◆●◆ ————

All of us had modeling assignments on the day of the big party. I had to sit in a classroom scene with five other models for a textbook ad. We were supposed to look bored. That was easy enough.

After we finished, I joined Nikki and Ashley in the Red Room to get ready for Ms. Calico's party. Ashley looked totally gorgeous in a dark green satin dress that came down straight to her waist and then flared out, with a wide black velvet ribbon at the dropped waist. Her blond curls were pulled back off her face and tied in a sleek ponytail with another black velvet ribbon. I would have felt like a dweeb in that outfit, but on her it was great.

"So, what do you think?" Ashley asked Nikki and me.

"You look beautiful," I said sincerely.

"Thanks," said Ashley. "Tonight my plan is to show Kate that I'm sophisticated enough to be the California Essence girl. They still haven't held the tryout yet. One of the ad execs got sick, so they postponed it."

"Good luck," Nikki said to Ashley. "You do look extremely sophisticated in that outfit."

Nikki also looked great in a crushed velvet A-line dress. It wasn't too green, either. It was mostly blue, with a thin green satin stripe running through it.

The only one who wasn't there was Chloe. But she came hurrying in the door, clutching a garment bag, just as I was stepping into my outfit—a one-piece black velvet jumpsuit with a tailored white blouse underneath. "I've never been so mortified in my life!" Chloe exclaimed.

"What happened?" Ashley asked.

"I was sent on a job today for Melville Laboratories," Chloe said. "Guess what it was for?"

"What?" Nikki asked.

Chloe took a deep breath, as if she could hardly bear to speak the words. "Children's cold medicine. That's for kids under twelve! Do I look that babyish?"

I studied Chloe. She had such delicate features that sometimes she did look younger than thirteen.

"Oh, no!" Ashley laughed.

Chloe wasn't smiling. "Grape-flavored kids' cold medicine. My baby sister takes that stuff. It's so embarrassing!"

"Looking young isn't so bad," Nikki said.

"Easy for you to say," Chloe said grimly. "You have those great long legs. Everyone thinks you're *older* than thirteen. I'll probably be doing little-kid toothpaste ads when I'm sixteen. Can you imagine what I'm going to have to put up with in school when that ad comes out? My life will be over."

"It's not that bad," Ashley disagreed matter-of-factly.

"Ashley!" Chloe cried. "I can't believe you, of all people, can say that. Look what you're going through over this California Essence ad."

"Sorry," said Ashley. "When you put it that way, I can imagine how you feel. But you don't look that young. You're just petite."

Chloe covered her face with her hands. "Oh, don't say that word!"

"Hurry up and get ready," Nikki said, changing the subject. "Renata said she's called limos to take the models to the party."

"You mean limo as in limousine?" I asked excitedly.

Nikki nodded. "I can hardly believe it, either. You know, when my friends Dee and Kathy talked me into entering the model search contest, Dee made me promise to take her for a limousine ride. I told her not to hold her breath because I'd never get into a limo. But this will be the second ride I've had in just a few months! I've got to find a way to get Dee into one of these limos."

As we talked, Chloe was pulling on a beautiful white dress with a swirling poinsettia print.

"I thought you were wearing green," Ashley said.

"You were so upset about it that I switched," said

Chloe. "My grandmother gave me this as an early present."

"Will she be there tonight?" I asked.

"No, she doesn't like parties," Chloe answered. "But my parents and Michelle will be. They really look forward to this party each year. The boys don't want to come, though, thank goodness."

When we were all dressed, we cracked open the door and peered down the quiet hallway. "The coast is clear," Ashley whispered, and we all scurried out.

"There you are!" Renata greeted us as we turned the corner. She looked like a holiday gypsy queen in a flowing dress of deep red and green with a sheer green shawl. "Hurry, hurry, hurry. Our limo driver is waiting. I'll ride with you girls."

Down on the street, we climbed into the long black car and nestled into the comfortable seats. A light snow began to fall as we left the city and drove over the bridge into the suburbs.

Ms. Calico lived almost an hour outside the city. When we turned off the highway, the houses grew larger and larger until they began to look more like mansions than houses. Finally the driver went down a dark road and made a turn up a steep hill.

I sucked in my breath and covered my mouth when Ms. Calico's house came into sight. It was almost unreal—a huge, square brick house set at the end of a long column of trees. Every tree and every window, door, and ledge were covered with twinkling white lights. It was like driving into a fairyland!

When we pulled up to the front door, I could hear jazzy, old-fashioned music playing inside. A man opened the limousine door for us.

"Isn't this awesome?" Nikki whispered to me as I fumbled in my bag for my sunglasses. She caught my arm. "Don't you dare put on those sunglasses. You'll look like some kind of nut."

"Oh, all right," I grumbled, knowing she was right. Still, I hated meeting all those people without them.

We stepped out of the limo just as a maid was opening the door. Inside, the hallway shone with dancing candlelight. I could hear people talking and laughing. Now I knew how Cinderella felt when she arrived at the ball—awed and scared out of her mind.

Chapter Nine

———◆———

Ashley!" Chloe cried. "Your brother is here! I'm going to die! Just die! He is *so* adorable. Why didn't you tell me he was coming?"

"I didn't know," Ashley replied.

I looked over their shoulders as we stood at the entrance to Ms. Calico's huge living room. It had high ceilings, and heavy maroon drapes were pulled back to reveal glistening windows with a zillion small panes. The white lights from outside twinkled through the sparkling windows, making the whole room glow. Or maybe the glow came from the blaze inside the stone fireplace, which took up an entire wall. All the women were dressed beautifully in sequined gowns and shiny dresses. It was like a picture in a magazine.

And across the room, standing by the fireplace, was Ashley's gorgeous mother, Taylor Andrews. I recognized her right away from her daily show, "Breakfast with Taylor." She was dressed in a stunning white suit, her long blond hair stylishly poufed. Beside her stood John Renee. His dark curls flowed down over the collar of his tuxedo. He looked just as handsome as he did on television.

"Where are my parents?" Nikki wondered.

"Is Eve coming?" I asked. Maybe I could sit in a corner and talk to her all night.

"Are you kidding? Eve is too intellectual and superior to go to a mere party. She's home with my brother Todd tonight, which is fine by me."

"I know what you mean," said Chloe. "My brothers would just find a way to embarrass me, too. Oh, there's Michelle."

Chloe ran off to greet her sister and I scanned the room, searching for any of the various members of my newly extended family. "There's your mom," said Nikki, pointing toward a long buffet table. "Is that her new boyfriend?"

"That's Mel," I said. "I'd better go see them." I crossed the crowded room. Mom looked pretty in a flowing blue dress with embroidery at the hem. Her hair was pulled back in a braid, and a pair of hammered silver earrings glittered in the firelight. I was proud of her appearance—cool and very individualistic. Mel wore a flattering loose-fitting suit.

"Hi!" Mom greeted me. "You look great." Mom and I had picked my outfit out of a catalog. Mom had even paid extra to have it shipped overnight.

"Thanks," I said. "So do you."

"Some party, huh?" said Mel, shifting on his feet. He clutched a cup of punch as if his life depended on it. "Good punch," he said, just to make conversation. "How are you feeling tonight, Tracey?"

From another person, that would have been a normal enough question, but coming from Mel, it made me want to scream. "I feel fine, thanks," I said stiffly.

"All this extravagant wealth doesn't make you uncomfortable?"

"No!" I said impatiently.

"Oh, well, good," he replied. "You know, just because a lot of these people have more money doesn't make them any better than you are."

"I know that!" I snapped. What did he think I was, an idiot?

"Tracey, there's no need to be so sharp," Mom said.

"Sorry," I mumbled. "Are Dan and Janine here yet?"

"I haven't seen them," said Mom.

I ladled a glass of punch from the large crystal bowl. Then I glanced toward the doorway and saw Dan and Janine come in. I wasn't the only one who noticed them. Everyone in the room seemed to. Dan looked really impressive in a tux, and Janine was dressed in a white pantsuit full of fringe and embroidery. With her long red hair spilling over one shoulder, she looked like a country-western star. "I'd better go say hi," I said, taking a quick sip of the punch.

As I weaved through the crowd, I almost bumped into Nikki. "That's my father and his wife," I told her.

"Wow!" said Nikki. "They look great. His wife looks like a country singer."

"Sort of," I agreed. "Come and meet them."

"I can't," she said. "My parents aren't here yet, so I offered to help Ms. Calico. She said to meet her in the kitchen."

I continued on to Dan and Janine. "Look at this beauty!" Dan said when I approached. I felt myself blush, but I was pleased by the compliment. "How did I get this lucky?" he went on. "I'm standing between the two most spectacular-looking women in the room."

Janine shoved him playfully and smiled. "Mr. Charm goes to the grand ball," she joked.

Despite her good humor, I could see that Janine was nervous. She kept clasping and unclasping her hands. I studied Dan to see how he was feeling. He had a smile on his face, but it seemed artificial. I wondered if it was an anxious smile—or even a drunken smile.

A fast look around showed me that Chloe was talking a blue streak to John Renee. Though he nodded politely, he appeared uninterested, as if he were talking to a little kid who was just babbling about nothing. I felt sorry for Chloe.

Ashley had cornered Ms. Calico. She was tossing back her head and laughing, a sort of hysterical, phony laugh. I think she thought it was a sophisticated laugh. Ms. Calico was staring at her quizzically, as if Ashley had lost her mind.

It didn't seem like Ashley's plan to prove her sophistication was going too well.

Ms. Calico broke away from Ashley and headed toward us. "That's her," I told Janine and Dan. "Ms. Calico."

"Hello, Tracey dear," Ms. Calico said when she reached us. She looked totally great, as always, in a short, dark purple dress. A spray of diamond earrings shimmered on each side of her face. "I wanted to come over and meet your parents."

Talk about your awkward moments! I was hoping I wouldn't have to get into a whole long explanation about who was who. But now there was no avoiding it.

"This is my father, Dan Morris," I said, "and this is his wife, Janine."

Gracious as ever, Ms. Calico didn't even blink. She simply shook their hands and greeted them. "Is your mother here?" she asked me after a minute.

I pointed Mom out to her. "Well, I'll go introduce myself," she said, then turned to Janine and Dan. "It was nice to meet you. I'm so glad you could come."

"She seems like a nice gal," Janine noted.

"I guess," I said. "Don't you think she's a little scary?"

Dan laughed hard. "I know exactly what you mean. She's a little too perfect. It seems kind of . . . unnatural. This whole place does. I have to admit I'm pretty uptight right now. I've never been in a place this fancy."

"Just relax," Janine told him.

He didn't seem drunk, only nervous, I decided. But I

did see waiters roving around the room with glasses of champagne on trays. I hoped Dan wouldn't use them to help get over his nervousness.

A waiter came along and offered us a bunch of different little snacks. I took a small hot dog rolled in a biscuit. As I munched on it I noticed that John Renee was sitting with Brittany Wells. I quickly looked for Chloe and saw her standing alone, wearing a terrible frown.

"Excuse me a moment," I said to Dan and Janine. "I have to go talk to someone."

"Sure, go on, honey," said Janine. "You don't have to stick with the old folks tonight. Have some fun."

I hurried across the room to Chloe. "I guess you and Ashley both hate Brittany Wells now," I said glumly.

"How can you hate her?" Chloe said miserably. "She's so sweet. But I wish I could hate her."

"She's just older, that's all," I said.

Chloe folded her arms and pouted. "Don't remind me. Once that children's cold medicine ad comes out, I won't have any chance with John at all."

"Where are your parents?" I asked to change the subject.

Chloe nodded over toward the buffet table. "They're comparing recipes with the caterer," she said. Sure enough, I saw Mr. Chang, looking like a giant, his arms flying around as he spoke to a short man who must have been the caterer. Mrs. Chang was talking excitedly, too.

Down at the other end of the table, Mel was pouring

himself more punch from the bowl. I suppose it gave him something to do while he waited for some unsuspecting victim to counsel.

Nikki joined us. "Don't worry, Chloe," she said. "John Renee will get bored with Brittany. She never says anything."

"Don't count on it," Ashley said, coming up behind Nikki. "Brittany could be the perfect girl for John since he loves girls who listen. He's a big talker."

"Oh, no!" Chloe wailed. "I was trying so hard to impress him that I never shut up for a second."

"Bad move," said Ashley. "But don't bother about him. I'm mad at him, anyway."

"Why?" I asked.

"Because he's Mr. Wonderful all the time," Ashley replied. "He just shows up unannounced, and my mother goes wild with happiness. He comes to the party and talks to my greatest rival, Brittany. I asked if he talked to his agent about me and he says yes, but the agent didn't get back to him yet."

"Those things aren't his fault," Nikki pointed out. "He probably has no idea how you feel about Brittany."

"Well, he should know," Ashley insisted irrationally.

"How could he?" Nikki challenged.

"He's my brother. He should know these things! On top of everything, he casually mentions that he spent the weekend with my father. They're so close, you'd think it was *his* father."

"I'm close to Martin," Nikki said. "Maybe that bothers Eve. I hadn't really thought of it that way before."

"Well, I'm sure that's not your fault," Ashley said. "John just bugs me sometimes."

"Brothers can be annoying," said Nikki. "But I still think he deserves a break."

"I'm not in a mood to be reasonable," Ashley groused. "I'm mad that he's on television and I'm not, that he saw my father and I didn't, and that my mother is making such a fuss over him. So let me be mad."

"You're right, he's a monster," Nikki said with a wry smile.

At that moment, an earsplitting crash made me whirl around. Everyone in the room stopped talking and turned toward the sound.

What I saw made me want to disappear on the spot. Dan was lying sprawled on the floor. All around him were the broken shards of a gorgeous vase that had been standing on a pedestal. Janine was trying to help him up, but he looked stunned. Or drunk!

"Your poor father," Nikki moaned. I didn't stop to hear anything else she might have said. I was too busy running.

I ran out of the room, out the front door, and along the walkway, down a sloping hill, into Ms. Calico's huge back lawn. It didn't take long before I reached some water that sparkled in the moonlight at the end of her yard.

When I stopped running, I realized I was freezing. I'd been so frantic to get out of there that I hadn't even stopped for my coat. To make matters worse, the tears on my cheeks felt as if they were freezing right on my face. I knew I'd have to go back inside. But I just couldn't. How could I face any of those people ever again?

In the moonlight, I saw a dock that jutted into the water. At the end of it was a small boathouse. If it was open, it might be warmer than standing in the cold. I headed toward it.

I was out on the dock, halfway to the boathouse, when I heard someone call my name. Even in the darkness, I recognized Dan's broad shoulders and his energetic, purposeful walk. I was desperate to get away from him— but not so desperate that I was about to jump into ice-cold water, which would have been my only way out. I had no choice but to wait for him there.

"I don't want to see you," I said hotly. "Please, just go away!"

"Tracey, please. I'm so sorry I embarrassed you, honey."

"Don't call me honey!"

"All right, but you've got to understand. I was heading over to talk to your mom when I stepped in some punch somebody spilled. My heel just spun out from under me, and the next thing I knew I was crashing into that fancy vase. It was an accident."

"Yeah, a drunken accident," I said, not facing him.

All I heard after that was silence. It lasted so long that I turned around slowly to see if he'd gone. But he was still there. "I haven't had a drink in a year," he said quietly. "Though I don't blame you for not trusting my word, after all you must have heard about me—after the way I've failed you."

"How can I trust you?" I began to yell. "I don't even know you. You're a stranger! I don't know what you would or wouldn't do. You're my father, but I don't know you at all. A kid shouldn't have a father who's a stranger. It's not right!"

As I spoke, I started to cry again. It was as if a dam had burst inside me and all the sad, angry, lonely feelings about not having a father had come rushing out. I couldn't stop crying.

As I covered my face and sobbed into my hands, I felt Dan drape his tuxedo jacket over my shaking shoulders. Then I felt his two strong arms enfold me as I drenched his white shirt with my tears. "It's all right, Tracey," he said soothingly. "It will all be okay. You'll see. I can't undo the past, but I can make the future better. I promise you, that's what I'll do."

Finally my tears stopped flowing and I got the hiccups. Dan looked down at me and smiled gently as he pulled a handkerchief from the pocket of the jacket I was now wearing. "Your aunt Maureen always hiccups after a good cry, too," he said, handing me the handkerchief. "I still can't believe how much like her you are."

I wiped my eyes and nodded. "I'd like to meet her someday."

"Someday you will," Dan said. "Right now, though, I'd like to go somewhere warm. It's freezing out here."

Even with his jacket on, I was still cold, too. Dan put his hand on my shoulder, and we began walking back up the dock. "I'm sorry for thinking you were drunk," I said.

"That's all right," he replied.

As we began walking on the grass toward the house, I heard Mel's voice cry out, "I think I see them, Caroline."

I took a tight, sharp breath and once again felt the strong urge to run away. I was in no mood for Mel right then. The last thing I wanted was to be cross-examined. I didn't want to go back to the party, either.

In the darkness, I saw Mel and my mother hurrying toward us. "Could we just bag this party and go back to your hotel?" I asked Dan.

"Sure, if it's okay with your mother," Dan said. "I'd like that."

"Me, too," I said. "Thanks, Dad."

Chapter Ten

Forget this modeling stuff," Dan said as we walked into his hotel room, where Janine lay on the bed watching a movie. "You should be an astronaut." We'd spent the last two hours down in the small video arcade in the lobby of the hotel, playing a game called Star Shooter. You had to blast attacking aliens out of the sky before they grabbed your fuel. Dan got better with each game, but I beat him every time.

"I've always thought about being an astronaut," I confessed, which was something I didn't tell many people. It took a lot of schooling to be an astronaut. I just didn't know if the money for school would be there. "It seems sort of far-fetched, though."

"Why not try for it?" Dan said, throwing his tux jacket on the bed. "You've got the brains and the guts."

"You think I've got guts?" I asked, pleased.

"I'm sure you do. All the Morrises have guts. Some of us have more guts than brains. But that's not something you have to worry about. You've got it all." I liked the way he was talking. He made everything seem possible.

"Maybe now that I'm modeling I can save some money for school," I said, feeling hopeful.

Dan's smile faded into a straight line. "You don't have to do it all yourself," he said after a moment. "I'm going to start living up to my responsibilities. You and your mother will be getting a check from me in the mail every month from now on. I'm not saying it will be a fortune, but I'll do the best I can."

I looked at him and nodded. My proud side wanted to say we didn't need his money, but the truth was, he owed us the money. He wasn't a stranger. He was my dad. It was his responsibility to help support me. It wasn't fair that Mom should have to do it all herself.

At that moment the phone rang and Janine picked it up. "Oh, hi, Stella," Janine said. "Yes, thanks for sending the outfit. I wore it tonight. How's my Gale? Good."

"Stella is Janine's sister," Dan told me. "She's watching the house and the dog for us until we return."

"When will that be?" I asked. I was so used to them that I'd almost forgotten they were leaving. Or maybe I just wanted to forget.

"We're going home this Wednesday," Dan said.

I looked at him and bit my lip. I didn't want him to leave. Not so soon. Not when I was starting to trust him.

"You know, Tracey, I want to be in your life now," Dan said. "Just because I'm going home doesn't mean you can't count on me."

"Yes, it does," I countered coldly. "That's exactly what it means."

"No, no. If you need me, I'll come in a snap. And you can visit me whenever you want. Janine and I have talked about that." He sat at the edge of the bed and took my hand in his own. "We also talked about asking you to come live with us, but we knew you wouldn't want to."

I'd never even thought of that possibility. Could I actually live with Dan and Janine? The idea seemed wild. But was it really that crazy? Janine was sweet and a lot of fun. There would even be a doghouse for Tuffy. Maybe they would let Tuffy in the house, since they slept with their own dog!

And Dan was my father. Little by little, that idea was seeming less strange.

It was as if Dan sensed these thoughts zooming through my brain. "I assumed that you wouldn't want to come live with us. Am I right about that?" he asked.

Instinctively I looked at Janine to see how she was taking this conversation. "It would be fine by me," she said.

"I would love to have you," said Dan. "We could try to make up for lost time. Of course, your mother would have to approve, since she has custody." He squeezed my hand and I squeezed back.

"I don't think I'd want to leave Mom," I said. "But it

means a lot to me that you'd want to have me."

"The day you come to live with us would be the happiest day of my life," said Dan.

The next morning, Dan drove me home, dropping me off in front of the apartment. I was surprised to find my mother crouching outside on the porch, wrapped in her old plaid flannel robe, feeding Tuffy some slices of ham. "He was scratching at the door," she said, glancing up at me. "He was looking for you."

"Thanks for feeding him," I said.

Mom stood up and pulled her robe more tightly around her. "It's cold. Let's go inside," she said.

We left Tuffy gobbling the ham and went in. "Listen, Tracey," Mom began. She didn't get to say any more, because at that moment there was a knock at the door. Mom answered. In walked the last person I wanted to see. Mel.

"How's it going this morning, Tracey?" he asked after kissing Mom hello.

"It's going fine."

"Did you straighten things out with your father?"

"Everything's cool."

"You know, Tracey," he began, "beating alcohol isn't easy. It takes a lot of personal courage. A recovering alcoholic needs the people in his life to have faith in him."

"So what are you saying?" I bristled. "Do you mean I let my father down by thinking he might be drunk?"

"I mean that having faith in people isn't always easy, but we have to do it for the sake of the people we care for."

"Oh, so if my father becomes a drunk again, it's my fault for not believing in him! Is that it?" I shouted. It really ticked me off that he was trying to dump that kind of guilt on me, especially when he didn't even know my father very well. Did he think all people were the same, that he had some kind of inside information about how all people would act in any situation?

"That's not what I said," Mel insisted in his super calm, counselor way. "All I meant was that to a recovering alcoholic who might still be in a delicate frame of mind—"

I hated this image of my father as some kind of mental cripple. "My father is not delicate-minded," I snapped. "If there's anyone who is, it's you! You stand around examining everybody, but you don't have half the guts my father has. You're just this guy who acts smart but doesn't know a thing about how people really—"

"That's quite enough, Tracey!" Mom cut in. "Mel is only trying to help you understand that—"

"That he's so superior to my father," I finished for her. "He's someone you can count on. Well, all I count on Mel for is to drive me crazy."

"That's it!" Mom said sharply. "Cut it out this minute! I will not have Mel insulted in this house."

"Mel's the one who's insulting my father!" I said angrily.

"Caroline, it's really all right. I understand where Tracey is coming from. She's been going through a lot with Dan's sudden reappearance in her life," Mel said calmly.

"You have no idea where I'm *coming from,*" I said, turning away from him. "You have no idea about anything!" With that, I stormed to my room, slamming the door behind me. I had never met anyone who bugged me as much as Mel. As far as I was concerned, there was only one good thing about him. He *wasn't* my father!

Not yet, anyway.

But what if Mom and Mel kept on dating? After a while, they very well might get married. The very thought made me shiver.

I pictured myself sitting down to endless rounds of cross-examination every evening. Every little move I made would be taken apart and examined for traces of antisocial behavior. It would be like living in a fishbowl. I saw myself as a goldfish looking out at Mel's big face staring in at me.

I couldn't think about it anymore. To push Mel out of my mind, I picked up a book and started reading. Luckily it was pretty interesting, so I could really lose myself in it. I love reading a good book, and I can keep on reading for hours. That's what I did all that day.

I was still reading early that evening when Mom knocked on the door. "Are you hungry?" she asked, sticking her head into my room.

I was starving, but I didn't feel like seeing her. "Not right now."

"All right," she said. "Listen, Tracey, Mel is only trying to help. You were very hard on him. It would be nice if you could apologize."

"He should apologize to me for always sticking his nose in my business," I said stubbornly.

Mom sighed in a sad, worn-out way. "I'm going out for a while. There's some frozen ziti in the freezer," she said. "You can just nuke it in the microwave."

"Sure, no problem." Somehow I couldn't imagine Janine being too busy to make dinner.

I kept reading until I fell asleep on the bed with the book open on my lap. I was awakened by the sound of the couple next door having an argument. They were just shouting at each other, but they were pretty loud.

Stretching, I stumbled out of bed and went into the kitchen. Mom still wasn't home. I opened the freezer and took out the box of frozen ziti.

I was putting the ziti in the microwave when I heard Tuffy whimpering outside. When I opened the door, I was hit by a blast of icy wind. Tuffy quickly scurried inside. "I can't leave you outside tonight," I said as I rubbed Tuffy to warm him up. Looking up at me with his big brown eyes, Tuffy licked my cheek. I really liked that little mutt.

With Tuffy in my arms, I plunked down in an easy chair. I could still hear the couple next door arguing. The only time their yelling was blocked out was when the fierce wind rattled the window frames.

As I petted Tuffy, I thought about how warm it must be in Arizona right now.

Chapter Eleven

On Monday I woke up with a stomachache. I was scheduled to go into the agency to discuss my Dingaling Cupcake ad with Ms. Calico. She met with every new model after his or her first solo shoot.

This would have been terrifying enough. But after what happened at the party, I couldn't face her.

There was another stomachache-making thing on my mind, too. Did I want to live with Dan and Janine? Somehow, during the night, the idea had grown more and more appealing. Or was it that the idea of someday having Mel for a stepfather had grown more and more horrible?

Up until yesterday, the very idea of leaving Mom would have seemed crazy. But now I saw how things would stand. Mel wouldn't stop trying to be my personal counselor. He would always drive me nuts. And Mom would always take

Mel's side. Somewhere along the line, he had become more important to her than I was. That alone filled me with a mix of anger and sadness.

Dan and Janine would be leaving in two days. It would be best if I made up my mind quickly. That way I could fly back with them. I was sure Mom would agree.

School that day went by in a blur. Afterward, I went straight to Nikki's house so Eve could drive me into the city.

I can never quite believe Nikki's family is for real. They remind me of one of those old-fashioned television families you see in black-and-white reruns. But even though I might make fun of her family, I secretly think it's sort of nice.

"Come on in," Nikki said when I knocked at her door.

"I see you're not going in," I said, noticing that she was wearing a blue sweat suit.

"Not today," she replied. We walked into her living room. Two girls were sitting with Nikki's ten-year-old brother, Todd. "These are my friends Dee and Kathy," she said, introducing us. "You met them during the contest at the mall."

"I remember. Hi," I said.

Kathy waved. Dee smiled at me, but she was busy playing a video game with Todd. "Ha! I beat you!" she said.

"Rematch! Rematch!" Todd cried.

"No, it's my turn to play the winner," Kathy said, moving off the couch onto the floor.

A plate of chocolate chip cookies sat on the coffee table. "Have a cookie," Nikki offered. "Mom made them."

"She bakes cookies?" I said in disbelief.

"They're just the kind you slice up and bake," Nikki explained.

"That's good enough for me," I said, taking a cookie. "My mother uses our oven to store the Christmas ornaments."

At that moment, Eve came downstairs and went to the coat closet. "I don't know how a person is expected to study with all that noise," she said irritably.

Nikki rolled her eyes. "Well, you're leaving now, so it doesn't matter."

Eve scooped a handful of cookies from the plate and headed for the door. "Come on, Tracey, let's go."

"Bye," I said with a wave as I hurried out the door after Eve. Most of the way in, Eve listened to her Chinese tapes. That was okay with me. I had a lot on my mind and didn't feel like talking.

"That will be fifteen dollars for gas, two for tolls, and the garage will probably cost me ten dollars," Eve said as she pulled up to the Calico agency.

"Twenty-seven dollars!" I cried.

"I'm not a charity worker," said Eve stiffly.

I paid Eve and got out. When I left the elevator, I gave the receptionist a quick wave as I walked past her, back to Ms. Calico's office. I'm not exactly sure when I stopped checking in with reception. Somehow it had just happened. I belonged there and everyone knew it.

When I neared Ms. Calico's office, I slowed down. A strong urge to run away had suddenly come over me. Then I felt a hand rest on my shoulder. It was Ms. Calico. She'd come from behind me.

"Hello, Tracey," she said. "Let's go right into my office." With her hand still on my shoulder, she walked me into her lovely wood-paneled office. On one wall was a couch with a coffee table in front of it. "Sit down and we'll go over these photos," she said.

"Ms. Calico," I said, my voice shaking, "I'm so sorry about the other night. I can't apologize enough for . . . I know you must be angry about . . ."

"About the vase?" Ms. Calico finished for me. "Nonsense. It is I who should apologize to your father. My staff should have wiped up that spilled punch. Your father was very gracious. Another person might have threatened to sue me."

"I still feel bad about the vase. If you want, you can take my modeling fees or—"

Ms. Calico held up her hand to stop me. "It's not necessary. Your father has already called and offered to pay, but I said absolutely not. Accidents happen, after all."

I couldn't believe how nice she was being!

"Now, let's look at these photos." She spread them out across the coffee table. There I was, eating a Dingaling pumpkin cupcake and—despite my true feelings—looking pretty thrilled about it. "Tracey, I don't know what to say," she said.

"Pretty bad, huh?" I said, picking up a picture.

"Bad?" she cried. "They're marvelous!"

"Huh?"

"You photograph wonderfully. I know your heart wasn't in it that day, but you surmounted that like a real professional. I see a great future in modeling for you, if you want it. You're a unique type, not run-of-the-mill at all. You will stand out."

If you want it. Did I?

"I have nothing to tell you, other than keep up the good work. Now that I see what your potential is, the agency will be sending you out on a lot more jobs."

"Thanks," I said, getting up from the couch. "And thanks for being so nice about the vase."

"Put it out of your head," she said.

I walked out of Ms. Calico's office feeling stunned. She'd really taken me by surprise. I was barely into the hall when Ashley came racing by me. Her eyes were filled with tears.

I'm not sure if she even saw me. Her head was down and she was moving fast. I could tell she was heading toward the Red Room, though, so I followed her.

I turned the corner just in time to see her duck inside the room. With a quick check over my shoulder to make sure no one else was in the hall, I went in, too.

"Ashley, what's wrong?" I asked. Her face was all puffed up from crying.

"At the party, after you left, Ms. Calico agreed to let me

interview for the California Essence ad campaign. I saw the people today, and they've already told me I didn't get the job. They said I'm too young!"

"Well, it's not like they said you're ugly or fat or anything like that," I pointed out. "Being too young isn't so bad."

I was trying to be helpful, but Ashley just began to sob. "Mom is going to Brazil, John is going back to California, and I'll be all alone with the housekeeper for the holidays."

"Why don't you just call your dad and tell him you want to see him?" I suggested.

"I don't know if he wants me to come. It's not like he's invited me."

Listening to Ashley got me thinking. Here she was upset because she wasn't sure her father wanted her to come see him.

I *was* sure my father wanted me to come.

Maybe that wasn't something to take lightly.

Something inside my heart shifted then and there. I knew what I needed to do. I was going to Arizona.

Chapter Twelve

———◆———

I felt as if I'd just punched Mom in the face. She was pale, and her hands started to shake. "Are you sure you want to go, Tracey?" she said in a shocked voice. "Have you given this enough thought?"

I nodded, but I couldn't meet her eyes. I didn't want to see the unhappiness there. "I think it would be . . . you know . . . better."

It would be better for everyone. I was sure of it. Mom didn't have a ton of money. Having me gone would be easier for her. She could also start her new life with Mel without a kid (namely, me) hanging around and getting in the way. I wouldn't have to put up with Mel, and I would have the kind of life I'd always dreamed about but would never admit I really wanted—a dad, a mom, a house, a dog. I would get to really know the father I'd never had. Everybody would be happier.

So why did I feel so horrible?

Still looking shocked, Mom sat on the couch. "This is very sudden, Tracey," she said. "What about school?"

"They have schools in Arizona."

"And modeling? And your friends?"

"I hardly ever see my friends in school anymore. I'll miss my friends from the agency, but I was never really sure about modeling, anyway. Dad says I can fly to Arizona with Janine and him this Wednesday."

"So I guess you've already spoken to him about all this," Mom said.

"Yeah. He's real happy about it," I said, unable to meet her eyes. "He was going to call you right away, but I told him I wanted to talk to you first."

"When did you say you wanted to go?"

"This Wednesday."

"That's two days from now!"

"There's no sense dragging it out," I said.

"I could just say no, and flat out forbid it," Mom said, as if she were talking to herself. "After all, I have legal custody. I'm in charge." She looked up at me, and her eyes seemed to search mine. I had to look away. "Why do you want to leave me?" she asked softly. "Is it because of Mel?"

In a way, it was. I didn't feel like getting into that, though. "No," I said.

"Let me talk to Dan," she said, getting up from the couch.

With a sigh, I went outside. The wind made me shiver

as I whistled for Tuffy. He came scampering across the courtyard and up the stairs right away. "How are you doing, pal?" I asked, rubbing behind his scraggly ears. "I guess you and I are going to be taking a trip soon."

Of course, he didn't know what I was saying, but he seemed to. He cocked one ear and looked at me with a puzzled expression.

A loose shutter banged in the wind. "In Arizona it will be warm all the time," I told Tuffy.

After a few minutes, Mom came out on the porch. Her face had a little color in it again, and she seemed calmer. "Your father really does want you to come," she said.

"I know that."

A piece of my hair blew across my forehead. Gently Mom brushed it away. "You're not my little baby anymore, are you?"

I shook my head. "It'll be all right, Mom. I'll call you and everything."

Mom nodded sadly. "You'd better see what you have to wear. Dan said he'd get you a plane ticket. You'd better call the Calico agency first thing in the morning."

"I have to go in with Nikki tomorrow, anyway," I told her. "The Dingaling people want to see me again for another ad. I'll have to tell them I can't do it."

"Are you sure you want to throw away your chance at a modeling career?" Mom asked.

"I just did it as a goof. I sure won't mind not having to eat another of their gross new cupcakes."

"All right, as long as you're sure."

Was I sure? I thought so.

The next day, Tuesday, Eve drove Nikki and me into the city after school. We had a little time to kill before our appointments, so we went to the Red Room. That's when I laid my bomb on her. I told her I was leaving for Arizona.

At first she didn't say anything. Then she started to laugh.

"I wasn't sure how you'd take the news but I didn't think it would drive you insane," I commented in confusion.

"What do you mean?" she asked through her laughter.

"Why are you laughing?"

"Because it's funny."

"No, it's not."

Slowly her face grew serious. "It's a joke, isn't it?"

"No. I'm really going to Arizona tomorrow."

"For how long?" Nikki asked.

"I don't know. Forever, I guess. Or until I find someplace better to be. You know."

Then Nikki ran through the same questions about school and modeling that my mother had. "Do you think this will make you happy?" she asked.

"Sure. Aren't you happy?" I asked.

"What do I have to do with this?"

"I want the kind of life you have, Nikki. I want the nice house and the family. I want to see what it's like not to eat frozen dinners all the time and live in an apartment that's one big dust ball."

"Your apartment isn't that bad," Nikki disagreed.

"You know what I mean."

"You're all wrong about my life," said Nikki. "Sure, I love my family. I even sort of love Eve, though I can't stand her. But we eat lots of frozen food, and my mom is at work all day and at law school part of the week. My house is neat because Martin is kind of a neat freak, and we all have these chores we have to do and—"

"I want chores!" I cried, surprising even myself. "Chores sound so family-like and cozy. I never had a chore in my life."

"You've never helped your mother?"

"Of course I have, but it's never like every Saturday we dust, and every Wednesday we change the sheets. We just do stuff when it occurs to us."

"So, that's all right."

"You don't understand," I mumbled. "You've always had that sort of order in your life."

Just then Chloe came in, looking jubilant. "Ask me what I got on my big history test," she said. "An A!"

"That's great," said Nikki quietly.

Instantly Chloe realized something was up. "I'm sorry," she said. "Were you guys having a serious discussion?"

"Tracey wants to go live with her father in Arizona," Nikki told her.

Chloe blinked, as if she didn't believe what she'd heard. "It must be hard to grow up without a father," she said after a moment.

Before I could say anything, Ashley practically burst into the room. "Oh, great! You're all here. I have big news. My dear, sweet, lovable brother John just heard from his agent, and he's going to arrange an audition for me next week. Next week! Can you believe it? I'll be flying out to California and I'll be there over Christmas!" She pumped the air excitedly, jabbing her fist above her head. "Yes! Yes!"

"That's cool," I said. "Congratulations. It seems like everyone is moving on."

"But *she'll* be coming back," Nikki said to me pointedly.

"Coming back?" Ashley questioned. "Naturally I'll be coming back. I'll be there for Christmas, and if I get the part, I'll either stay or go back again. It's just what I wanted. Who needs some stinky old perfume ad, anyway?"

Nikki told Ashley about my decision. I thought that if anyone would understand, it would be Ashley. I was wrong.

"You're making a big mistake," she said bluntly. "You're going to ditch modeling? Just like that?"

"It's her life," Chloe argued with Ashley.

"Yeah, but do you know how many opportunities modeling opens up for you? Do you realize how many girls want to be in your shoes, Tracey? You must have gumballs in your head instead of brains. I don't care how smart you may be."

"There's more to life than modeling," I said angrily.

"Maybe so, but modeling can sure be great. You haven't even given it a chance," Ashley replied.

I didn't like the way this conversation was going. It wasn't making things easier. Luckily I had to meet with the Dingaling people. "See you guys later," I said as I left the Red Room.

My meeting with the Dingalings didn't go too well, either. Ms. Cosgrove and Muffy Addams were waiting for me in the conference room when I walked in with Renata. "There's my girl," said Muffy, as if I were her long-lost daughter. "The Dingaling execs are all wild for your ad. We must have another as soon as possible. I see big things in your future. You can have a career as the Dingaling girl!"

When I thought of my future life, I definitely didn't see myself as the Dingaling girl.

"I'm sorry," I said. "I won't be able to do another ad for you."

Ms. Cosgrove's pudgy hand flew to her heart. "Why on earth not?"

"Because I'm giving up modeling."

"What?" Renata gasped.

"You're not serious!" cried Ms. Cosgrove.

Muffy jumped to her feet. "You'll never eat another cupcake for Dingaling!" she threatened.

Part of me wanted to laugh at that. But another part felt like crying. I guess you never realize how much you're going to miss a Dingaling cupcake until it's gone.

Chapter Thirteen

Are you ready?" Mom called from outside my bedroom door.

"One minute," I called back. I wanted to take one last look around my room. Not that it was so great. But it had been mine, and I would miss it.

It was Wednesday morning. I was due to meet Dan and Janine at the airport at noon. Dan had my ticket, and Janine had even bought me a special carrying case for Tuffy.

Ms. Calico hadn't been in the office the day before, but Renata said she'd talk to her for me. Renata said that the Dingaling cupcake ad made us even for the thousand-dollar advance the agency had paid me, and she didn't see any problem with getting out of my contract. I was glad Ms. Calico hadn't been there. I couldn't have faced her.

In the living room, the phone rang. "It's for you," Mom said.

I came out of my room and took the phone from her. "I just called to say, you know, so long and all," said Nikki. "I wasn't sure if you had my address, either. You're going to write to me, aren't you?"

"If you want. Sure," I said. I was glad she'd mentioned writing to each other. It somehow made saying good-bye less painful.

It wasn't until that exact moment that I realized how much I would miss Nikki—and Chloe and Ashley, too. Without my noticing, they'd come to mean a lot to me.

"I'll write you a postcard as soon as I get there," I said. "Which will be today, so you'll be hearing from me soon."

"Good," said Nikki. "Oh, and Eve told me to give you a message, but I can't remember it. It was in Chinese. I think it meant good luck and be happy. That goes for me, too."

"Thanks," I said. "Well, I'll see you."

"Come on, we have to go," Mom told me. "Mel is waiting for us outside."

"Mel is taking us to the airport?" I questioned.

"Yes," said Mom. "I didn't want to be . . . I thought I'd like a friend along."

"Sure," I said. "I understand." I could see how important Mel had become to her. She wouldn't miss me for too long.

Just as we were almost out the door, the phone rang again. It was Ashley. "Are you really doing this?" she asked.

"Yes, and I have to go," I said. "But thanks for calling."

"I called to try to talk some sense into you," Ashley said.

"My mind is made up."

"When's your flight?" she asked.

"One-thirty."

"What airline?"

I told her and she gasped. "I wouldn't fly that airline if my life depended on it. They are the worst. Trust me. My family flies all the time. You'd better not set one foot on that plane."

"Nice try, Ashley, but it's a major airline."

"So? The *Titanic* was a major ocean liner! It still sank!"

"Bye, Ashley. I'll miss you," I said, gently hanging up.

I scooped up Tuffy from where he was sleeping on the couch and headed out the door with Mom. Suddenly I realized I'd forgotten something very important. My sunglasses!

"I'll be right back," I told Mom as I passed Tuffy to her. I ran back to the apartment and grabbed my glasses off the kitchen table. I knew that today I would need them for sure. If I started to cry, I didn't want anyone to see.

Once again, the phone rang. "I just heard what airline you're taking," Chloe said when I picked up. "Don't do it. People call the staff the Crash and Burn Crew. The flight attendants never take off their life preservers. They can barely get down the aisles, but they're too scared to take them off. You're too young to die, Tracey!"

"I guess you've been talking to Ashley," I said.

"Yes, well, when she mentioned the name of the airline, I had to call you immediately."

"I like to live dangerously, Chloe," I said.

"I tried, anyway." Chloe sighed. "Good luck."

"Same to you. So long." I hung up the phone and smiled sadly. I was glad they didn't want me to leave, even if their way of getting me to stay was a bit weird.

I went back outside and locked the apartment door behind me. Mom and I walked quietly to Mel's car. It was the first time I'd seen him since I'd yelled at him. I felt nervous about it, but he just acted as if nothing had happened. I guess when you have a personality as annoying as Mel's, you get used to people being ticked off at you.

"Hi, Tracey," he said.

"Hi," I said dully as I climbed into the backseat. I knew I was being sort of bratty. Maybe Mel wasn't the worst guy on earth. He meant well—I just couldn't stand him.

For the most part, we didn't speak on the ride to the airport. Mom and Mel listened to the radio. I petted Tuffy and tried to keep him calm. I don't think he'd ever been in a car before. He sat with his head buried in my lap the whole time.

Janine and Dan were waiting for us at the departure gate. My spirits lifted when I saw their smiling faces. "Ready for the big flight?" Dan asked me.

"Yep," I said.

Janine took Tuffy from me. "Hi there, you little cutie," she said to him. "We have a nice warm doghouse ready and waiting for you. Though if you're like my Gale, you'll never see the inside of it."

An announcement came over the P.A. system. "Passengers for flight seven-oh-five departing for Phoenix may begin boarding at gate twelve now."

A panicky look swept across Mom's face.

"We have time," Dan said kindly.

Mom shook her head. "Excuse me, then. I need to find a ladies' room. I'll be right back."

"So, I hear you're in computer repair," Mel said to Dan, filling the awkward silence after my mother left. "That's always sounded interesting to me." Dan and Mel went on to chat about fixing things, while Janine played with Tuffy. I put on my sunglasses and stared around the airport, taking in the sights.

Another announcement about flight 705 came over the loudspeaker, and I checked the clock on the wall. "Where is your mother?" asked Dan.

"I'll go find her," I offered. Remembering that the ladies' room was just down the hall, I started off.

I was running along the corridor when I stopped short. Coming toward me at a gallop were Chloe, Ashley, and Nikki. "There she is!" Ashley cried as they continued charging toward me.

"Gee, you guys didn't have to come all the way down here to say good-bye," I said, even though I was really touched that they had.

"That's not why we came," Ashley panted. "We came to stop you. Tracey, you can't do this. We were all talking about you, and we suddenly realized something."

"What?" I asked.

"That you're crazy," said Ashley.

"What?" I yelped.

"Ashley means that your ideas about families are crazy," Chloe said. "You're looking for a family no one has. You won't have it in Arizona, either. Janine and Dan have busy lives. They won't be there waiting on your every need. Right now they're on vacation, but once they get home, they'll get back to their jobs. They'll be overworked and get crabby sometimes, just like all our parents do."

"But you all have real families," I objected.

"So do you," said Nikki. "You have your mom. Until your father showed up, you and she were really close."

"Until Mel showed up, you mean," I said.

"Tracey!" Nikki cried in exasperation. "I met Mel at the party. He's not that bad. You have to give him half a chance. I didn't like Martin all that much when I first met him. In fact, I couldn't stand him."

"You couldn't?" I asked. "But you love Martin."

"*Now* I love Martin, but not at first," said Nikki. "I thought he was this stuffy, know-it-all lawyer. Part of him is, but he has a lot of good parts, too."

"I'll bet anything that you'll want to come home in a few days," said Ashley. "And by then, you'll have thrown away your whole modeling career. Ms. Calico doesn't take girls back once they quit."

"Don't go," Chloe said. "We'll miss you too much. And you might not realize it now, but you'll miss us, too."

She was right. I would miss them, probably more than I imagined. "How did you guys get here, anyway?" I asked.

"I called a limo," said Ashley. "My mother has a corporate account. She'll have a fit when she sees that I used her account number, but this was an emergency."

No, I wasn't going to find friends like this again too easily.

Just then, another announcement filled the air. "Passengers for flight seven-oh-five for Phoenix should be boarding at gate twelve."

"I have to find my mother," I said quickly. "You guys wait here, okay?"

I raced down the hall until I got to the bathroom. When I stepped into the white-tiled room, I didn't see her. "Mom?" I said. "Are you here?"

I looked below the stalls and saw only one pair of legs. They belonged to my mother. "Mom, are you okay?"

Then I heard the sound of sniffling.

"Mom, can I come in?" I called at the metal door. The door swung open. There stood my mother, her face blotchy and red, her eyes swollen with tears.

"I'm sorry, Tracey," she said with a sniff. "I didn't mean to do this. Honestly I didn't."

Mom wiped her eyes with the back of her sleeve and blew her nose with some toilet tissue. She squeezed me tight and then pulled away. "Come on, let's go," she said.

She gathered her jacket off the door hook, and we left the stall. On the way out, she stopped by a sink and splashed water on her face. Another announcement came on about flight 705. This one sounded urgent. Mom and I jogged down the hall.

As I hurried behind her, I noticed something that was typically Mom. "Mom, your sweatshirt is on inside out," I said, jogging up alongside her.

She stopped and looked at the exposed seams of her shirt. Shaking her head, she laughed sort of sadly. "What a flake!" she chided herself.

"Don't say that, Mom!" I cried. "You're not a flake at all."

Pictures of my life with Mom swept into my head. I remembered hiking with her on summer days. I remembered the time she'd sold our car so we could have a vacation at the seashore together, and how all that fall she'd stood out at the bus stop waiting for the bus to take her to work. I remembered how we'd huffed and puffed our way to the top of a mountain on my tenth birthday. "I don't have money to give you a big present, Tracey," she'd said. "But I can show you this view, and no one can ever take that away from you."

Just then, Mel, Dan, and Janine rushed down the hall toward us. "We've got to board now," said Dan.

"I'm not going," I said. "I'm sorry, but I can't."

Dan checked his watch. Then his aqua eyes flashed between Mom and me. "You're sure?"

I nodded.

He gently drew me off to one side, where we stood

among a bunch of empty seats. "You know, Tracey, as much as I want you to come, I think you're making the right choice. I sat up thinking about it all last night. I was afraid that we were both rushing things. You and I are still getting to know each other. We have the rest of our lives to do that. How about coming out for a visit this summer?"

I nodded. "That's probably a smart idea."

"We'll take one step at a time. I'll write and call. And you can always call me collect if you need me."

I hugged him tight, and it felt so natural. "I'm glad you came to find me," I said honestly.

"It would have been my loss if I hadn't," he said. He hugged me hard. Then we walked back to the others. "We've got to go," he said to Janine.

Janine gave me a quick kiss on the cheek and handed Tuffy to me. "Bye, hon. We'll be in touch."

Nikki, Tracey, and Chloe joined us as we watched them hurry off down the hall toward the gate. I wrapped my arm around my mother's waist, and she put her arm around my shoulder. We stood there together, watching Dan and Janine disappear, and I knew I was where I belonged.

Chapter Fourteen

━━━━◆━━━━

Are you serious?" I asked Renata the following Monday. "You really didn't tell her I was quitting?"

"Yes, I'm serious," Renata said with a smile. "I had a very strong feeling that you'd be back, so I decided it wouldn't hurt to wait a few days to tell Kate you'd be leaving."

Whew! I'd come all the way into the city to beg Ms. Calico to take me back. Now I wouldn't have to. What a relief!

It made me wonder about Renata. Maybe she *was* psychic. "Thanks a lot," I told her.

"No problem, Tracey," she said. "I'm glad you're back."

So was I. If I hadn't almost left, I might not have realized how much I'd come to like this place. Even if modeling wasn't my deepest ambition, it was interesting. I was meeting so many different kinds of people. The thought of returning to a life without modeling suddenly seemed hopelessly dull.

I stepped out of Renata's office into the hallway. Almost instantly, Ms. Calico swooped down on me. "Tracey, I need a word with you," she said.

"Sure," I agreed a bit anxiously.

"The way you handled those Dingaling people last week—telling them you were quitting modeling—was quite unprofessional. If you didn't want the job, you should have told them so honestly. Being temperamental will ultimately work against you in this business."

"But . . . I . . ." I stammered. What could I say? I didn't want Ms. Calico to know that I really had meant I was quitting modeling when I said it. "I'm sorry, Ms. Calico."

"It's all right, dear. I've worked everything out with them. In fact, as it turned out, telling them that you weren't modeling anymore only made them wild to have you. After Muffy Addams calmed down, she called me and offered three times the money they were originally paying."

"She did?"

"Yes. You got away with it this time, but she could have just as easily told other clients not to work with you because you're too difficult. So keep a check on that temper in the future. You don't want to ruin your modeling career, do you?"

"No, I don't," I said, and I meant it.

She patted my shoulder and went into her office.

A slow smile spread across my face. Today was turning into a very good day.

Sunday had been a very good day, too. Mom and I went to the movies together. Then we met Mel afterward at an Italian restaurant where they made great lasagna. Once I relaxed around Mel, I discovered he wasn't such a bad guy. And he must have gotten my message, because he didn't ask me a single personal question. Without his probing counselor routine, I would have to say I actually liked him.

When we got home, Mom had a surprise for me. In my room was a small, round dog bed. "I haven't seen that landlord around here in two years," Mom said. "I don't know what I was so worried about."

I hugged her hard.

Now, since I didn't have to plead for my modeling contract back, I had time to kill before Eve came to pick Nikki and me up at six. I decided to finish my homework in the Red Room.

Chloe and Ashley were already there, flipping through a magazine. "How did it go with Kate?" Ashley asked.

"Renata never told her I was leaving."

Ashley nodded knowingly. "I told you Renata has a gift. She really knows stuff."

At that moment, it was hard to argue with her.

"What are you looking at?" I asked, kneeling down on the floor beside them.

"We're trying to figure out what stars Ashley might run into when she gets to Hollywood. She'll meet all those cute guys from 'One Ashford Avenue,' of course," said Chloe. She sighed longingly. "I wish I was going."

Ashley's eyes went wide as she was struck with an idea. "Maybe they need extras or something. Maybe you guys could come with me."

"I don't think your father would want three extra houseguests for Christmas," Chloe pointed out.

"No, I suppose you're right," Ashley agreed. "But I'll go there and check it out. If I can come up with something for all of you, I'll call after the holidays. Wouldn't that be a blast?"

"It would be so cool!" Chloe agreed.

"What airline are you flying?" I asked Ashley.

When she told me, I put my hands on my hips and looked at her sternly. "Isn't that the flying *Titanic* that you told me not to take?"

Ashley glanced at me guiltily. "We had to try something. We just couldn't let you make such a huge mistake."

"Thanks," I said.

Nikki came in, holding a brown paper bag. "I got them," she said happily.

"What's in the bag?" I asked.

One by one, Nikki lifted four tall paper cups from the bag and set them on the floor. "Chocolate milk shakes!" she announced.

"I really shouldn't," Ashley said. "These are way too fattening."

"And they're terrible for my skin," added Chloe.

"Are you guys serious?" I asked.

"We are models," said Ashley. "We have to take things like this seriously."

"Then I'll drink all of them," I said.

"No way!" cried Nikki, grabbing my arm. Chloe and Ashley each snapped up a milk shake, too.

"I think we should make a toast," said Ashley, lifting her milk shake into the air.

"To what?" asked Nikki.

"To friendship," I said.

"To friendship," my friends sang out as we tapped our cups together. Then we slurped down our shakes. Somehow a chocolate milk shake had never tasted sweeter than that one did, there in the warm glow of the Red Room.